UR~~CELIA~~
TEIXEIRA

A JORJA ROSE CHRISTIAN THRILLER

VALLEY OF DEATH SERIES BOOK 3 OF 3

WAGES
OF SIN

WAGES OF SIN

A JORJA ROSE CHRISTIAN SUSPENSE THRILLER

VALLEY OF DEATH BOOK III

by URCELIA TEIXEIRA

Copyrighted material
E-book © ISBN: 978-1-928537-82-3
Paperback © ISBN: 978-1-928537-83-0
Independently Published by Urcelia Teixeira
First edition

Urcelia Teixeira, Wiltshire, UK

www.urcelia.com

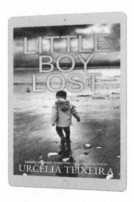

To our squishy cat, Gadget:
For keeping me company, for
keeping my feet warm during those cold winter days,
and for stealing my chair every time I took a bathroom
break.
Couldn't have done it without you, buddy!

INSPIRED BY

"He has delivered us...and transferred us to the kingdom of His
beloved Son, in whom we have redemption, the forgiveness of sins."
Colossians 1:12-14
(ESV)

CHAPTER ONE

J orja sat alone in the quiet room inside the British Consulate in Abu Dhabi. She no longer felt any emotions, nor did she know if she ever would again.

Numbed by the unexpected turn of events and mourning Ben, whom she was certain Sokolov had already killed by now, she stared at the disposable cup of cold coffee they had placed in front of her hours ago.

She had not seen or heard from Pascale since his men took her away and locked her inside the room, and she had long since given up thinking that she'd walk out of there a free woman.

Where she sat at a table in the middle of the small room, staring out of the tiny rectangular window at the very top of the wall, she watched the sun's rays grow brighter as it announced the start of the new day. It had been days since she slept, not that she cared much any longer. Nothing mattered anymore. Everyone she had ever loved and cared for had been stripped away from her, even the person she once was.

She had tried talking to God, searched for answers, the truth. But instead, she had found her heart hardened and her spirit angry with Him. She had thought that she could trust Him, that He was helping her. But even that wasn't to be.

Her mind trailed to the words she had clung to before it all began, but this time, it brought her nothing but pain. She had been in a valley of the shadow of death, feared evil, faced it head-on, remained in its cold grip, yet she no longer sensed God anywhere.

Had He forsaken her because she had sinned? Perhaps she was wrong to think He should help her in the first place. Whatever it was, it was clear.

She would pay for her sins for the rest of her days.

Caught up in her agony, her mind trapped in another dimension, she jumped when the door suddenly shut beside her. When she turned to find the person who had entered, she saw that it was one of the officials who had briefly popped in to drop off her luggage. She had left it at the hotel in Geneva. How was it that they had found it? Why was it there?

Her heart bolted as a million questions rushed through her mind and she recalled the files she had hidden inside. When the official left, she shot across the floor to pick up her suitcase, lifted it atop the desk and moved to open it.

"Don't bother, it's not there anymore."

Pascale was suddenly behind her, his face warm and inviting like the day she had sat next to him on the plane.

"I don't know what you're talking about," she lied, her heart guarded.

"Take a seat, Jorja. We have a lot to discuss."

"I have nothing to say to you."

"Oh, I'm sure you do, but even if I believed that, there is a lot I have to say to you. So, please, sit down."

She did, watching him move the suitcase back onto the floor before he sat down opposite her and placed a folder on the table in front of him.

Jorja shuffled nervously in her seat.

"I want legal representation. I've been asking for one since you brought me here. I know my rights. You can't keep me here."

"You won't need any if you cooperate with us."

"Cooperate with you? And do what exactly? You already got what you wanted, so what's left? I'll tell you what's left, the bitter taste of betrayal."

She crossed her arms and stared blankly out the small window.

"Fair enough, you have every right to be angry. But I have a right to explain my side also."

"No, you don't. Nothing you can say will fix this, Pascale. You played me, used me, and now Ben is dead. And it's all thanks to you. We had a deal and you didn't honor it. But I guess you knew you weren't going to right from the start. So, I guess the joke's on me."

Pascale didn't argue. Instead his fingers tapped at his cell phone, holding it up for her to watch something on the screen.

When she looked she saw Ben, his face badly beaten, his voice strained when he spoke.

"Jorja, it's me. I'm told you're okay. I'm fine too. I knew you could do it. Then again, you learned from the best." He laughed, then flinched when his smile pulled at a wound on his lips. "Anyway, I can't wait to see you and hear all the details. Hopefully, that will be soon." He blew her a kiss before the video shut off.

A soft sigh escaped from Jorja's quivering lips.

"I want to see him." Her voice was soft and laden with emotion when she spoke.

Pascale placed his phone face-down to one side of the table and clasped his hands on top of the folder in front of him.

"I would like nothing more than to take you to him but I'm afraid it isn't possible right now."

"Why not?"

"Well, for a start, he's in the infirmary. He took quite a beating."

"Even more reason for me to see him. Please, I need to see Ben."

"He hasn't been properly processed."

"Processed? What for? He's done nothing wrong."

"The man's been on the wanted list for more than two decades, Jorja. He's breached dozens of cyber laws in just about every country in the world. It's out of my hands now."

Jorja placed her palms on the table and leaned in toward Pascale. "Ben walked away twenty years ago, Pascale. It's my fault he got involved. We didn't have a choice. I didn't have a choice. And Ben nearly died in all of this. Lock me up and throw away the key for all I care, but you have to let him go. Please. You got what you wanted. Just let him go."

Her eyes were suddenly watery and her voice desperate and pleading as she stared into Pascale's questioning eyes. Caught by surprise at the sour expression that flashed across Pascale's face, she backed away and retreated into one of the corners of the room to take hold of the emotions that raged inside her.

When Pascale spoke, something in his voice had changed. It had lost the taint of compassion he spoke with mere moments ago.

"If he means that much to you, I'll see what I can do to cut him a deal of some sorts, but first you and I have to come to an arrangement."

Jorja crossed her arms and leaned back against the wall as she scoffed. "So now you're blackmailing me again."

"That's not quite how I would describe it. May I remind you that you broke the law, Jorja? I'm offering you an opportunity to not go to prison."

"You tricked me, deceived me into stealing that painting! It's entrapment, is what this is. I want a lawyer."

But her words had no impact on Pascale and she watched him hang his jacket over the back of his chair before he pushed his sleeves up and opened the folder.

"Take a seat, Jorja. I hate to have to do this but you have run out of options. The way I see it, we need you as much as you need us, so the quicker we get this done, the sooner we can all go on with our lives and you and Ben can drive off into the sunset together when he one day gets out of prison." His voice broke as he spoke the words before he cleared his throat to continue. "What I'm offering you is complete immunity in exchange for your skillset and cooperation in taking the *Gardiens* down." He paused, his head bowed as he waited for Jorja to respond.

Confusion and anger left Jorja pacing between the corners of the room, her palms flat against her temples as she struggled to make sense of it all. Questions flooded her mind. Why was he doing this to her? Why was he forcing her to sin by blackmailing her into working undercover with him? And why was he so bothered by her wanting to see Ben? If she didn't know any better she'd swear Pascale was jealous. How dare he? He had no right to toy with her emotions like that. Before, when he tricked her, he had used his charm to rope her in, but now ... now there was no logic to why he needed her. After all, he was an Interpol agent with all the resources he would ever need to succeed, and he was married to a woman who was quite obviously involved with the *Gardiens*. He already had everything at his disposable to take them down.

The reminder of his association with the *Gardiens* had her recalling the tattoo she'd seen on Pascale's arm and she found herself glancing back at his exposed arms on top of the table.

"It's fake," Pascale said when he realized what she was looking for.

He had caught her by surprise and she quickly turned away from him.

Jorja's reaction stung at Pascale's insides. She had every reason to be angry with him. She was right. He had used her. The same way he had taken every opportunity available to him over the past decade in his mission to take down the *Gardiens*. He was desperate, but more than that, he had let his guard down and allowed her to mess with his head—and his heart.

CHAPTER TWO

Annoyance tugged at Pascale and soon pushed him to his feet. Where he now stood behind his chair, his hands resting on the backrest, he dropped his head, desperate to find a way forward.

"You're right. I used you. But, to be fair, it was pure coincidence that you got caught in my crosshairs. It just so happened that our paths crossed and I took the opportunity to do my job."

He pushed himself away from the chair and placed both hands on his hips, his head bowed as if he were ashamed when he continued.

"You have every right to be angry with me Jorja. I did deceive you, but only because I didn't have a choice either."

Pascale's voice seemed sincere and from his droopy shoulders and downward stare at his hands that now gripped the back of his chair again, Jorja guessed Pascale was battling an inward torture of his own. She slowly walked toward her chair and sat down across from him again. When he looked at her, something in his eyes evoked compassion for his circumstances and she spoke in a soft voice. "If I help you, you have to let Ben go."

Pascale's eyes narrowed as he looked up, the muscles in his jaw tense as if he was holding back a question—or holding all the cards. Unable to read the expression on his face, she tried again.

"Ben is like a brother to me, Pascale. He's all I have left in this world. I will never be able to forgive myself if he has to spend the rest of his life behind bars. I'll do whatever you need me to do if you keep him safe and out of prison. You have my word."

There was a long pause.

"I'll be back in a bit," Pascale finally spoke, then turned and left the room, taking the folder with him.

Left alone in the room, Jorja turned her attention back to the sunlight that poured through the tiny window and suddenly lit up the entire room around her. It was as if a heavy cloak of darkness had been lifted away to make space for a warm blanket of peace that now wrapped snugly around her shoulders. She closed her eyes, pushed her chin out toward the light, and thanked God for saving Ben.

Even though her future was yet to be determined, even if she was still confused as to why God had allowed her to be in this position, she found peace in knowing that her indiscretions wouldn't be the cause of pain on the lives of any more innocent people. Her wrongdoings had caught up with her. Every last one of them, and perhaps this was how she was meant to pay for it. Sacrificing the life she had always dreamed of living, her home in St. Ives, her beloved cat, Vincent, the hope of one day having someone to love and grow old with, it would all be worth losing if in return she atoned for her sins. She would take her punishment and claw her way through it to where she would hopefully, eventually, find rest for her weary soul. Even if it were to be in prison.

The door shut noisily beside her when Pascale re-entered the room to take his seat again

Jorja snapped back into the present. She watched as he placed the folder back in its place on the table in front of him then leaned forward. Jorja's eyes widened with expectation as he spoke.

"I've had a word with my superior. In exchange for your full cooperation, they will grant Ben complete immunity. He will get a new identity and be relocated to an undisclosed location where he will be contractually committed to putting his skills to use for us, whenever we might need them."

He paused to study Jorja's face as she realized what that meant. "Unfortunately, that also means you won't have any contact with each other from here on out for fear of compromising his association with Interpol. Not to mention the high risk it poses given your history together."

Jorja slumped back in her seat and loosely folded her arms across her chest. A single tear trickled down her cheek. She had walked out on Ben twenty years ago, at peace with never seeing him again. She could do it again if it meant he'd be free. She at least owed him that much for nearly getting him killed.

She nodded as she wiped her tears on her sleeve. "What do you need?"

Pascale's heart ached with what he had to do. Perhaps one day she could come to forgive him for forcing her hand, for using her. But he had given up too much to let all his work infiltrating the *Gardiens* go to ruin. He had lost a lot too.

It took Pascale a few seconds to reply. "I'm not going to lie to you, Jorja. Heaven knows I've done enough of that. So I'm going to give it to you straight. It's not going to be easy. The road ahead will be tough and possibly require far more than what you are prepared to give, but we believe you are the only one equipped enough to get us to the finish line. Frankly, we thought Nikki was the one for the job, but you have far outweighed her abilities and proven your worth in getting the *Salvator Mundi*. Had it not been for that painting, we would have hit a dead end. We have been at it for nearly a decade and it's the closest we've ever come to taking down the *Gardiens*."

Jorja fell silent once Pascale had finished. It was a lot to take in. When she looked up she fixed her eyes on his.

"And once I deliver my side of our deal, will you grant me the same immunity?"

"Provided the mission is successful, yes."

Jorja scoffed. "Sounds like a raw deal no matter which way you slice it."

"We have the full backing of every single international government department and their resources. You've met and worked with the team. You will work with them again —barring, of course, Nikki, who won't ever see another day outside her prison walls. I knew she was a risk, but I give you my word you will have my full support, Jorja—and protection." Pascale leaned in. "Just don't double-cross us like Nikki did and you'll be fine." His lips curled into a playful smile.

"And where exactly do you fit into all of this, Pascale? If that is even your real name."

Pascale leaned back in his chair, his hands resting on his knees before he vigorously rubbed at them.

"I guess you're right. If we are going to be working together I owe you an explanation and a bit more information." He got up and walked to press a single red button next to the door, then glanced up to see if the overhead camera that had been recording the entire time had switched off. When he was satisfied they had total privacy, he took his seat again.

"My name is Pierre Pascale Laurent. Lupin is a nickname my colleagues gave me a long time ago when I first started undercover work in the International Art Crimes division, a comical play on the fictional character for his knack of using various disguises. I go by Pascale Lupin when I'm working—it's easier. We became aware of the Bouvier corporation's involvement in the *Gardiens* nearly ten years ago, but could never gather enough evidence to take down either of them. We needed someone on the inside." Pascale shuffled uncomfortably in his seat. "It seemed the only way in was through Gabrielle Bouvier." He briefly looked away as he said her name then fixed his eyes on Jorja's when he continued. "She's not my wife. We're not legally married. We're not even in a relationship. She's a smokescreen, part of my cover in an arrangement we had made with her after her father passed away. When Jacques Bouvier died, he left her a document in which he exposed Gerard Dubois and confessed to his involvement with him. At the time I had already entered into my assignment—we were dating so, naturally, she confided in me. I took the opportunity to use the document as evidence, but the information wasn't solid enough to get a conviction that would stick to Gerard —he's as crafty as they come. We saw an opportunity and took it. Gabrielle agreed to help infiltrate the *Gardiens* if we kept her father's improprieties from being exposed. The Bouvier corporation would have gone up in smoke and she would have lost everything. The mutual arrangement suited us both and we've been working at it ever since. Finding the *Salvator Mundi* and using it as bait was the closest we'd ever come to taking Gerard down, and Gabrielle has agreed to let us keep it in play."

"There's only one problem, though," Jorja said.

"I'm listening."

" You are compromised. Your cover is blown. By now Sokolov has made it his mission to get word out about you to Gerard. Trust me. In the illicit world of high-ticket art, these criminals all know each other and Artem Sokolov would have undoubtedly used this piece of information to his advantage."

A faint smile broke on Pascale's lips. One that was equally triggered by how impressive her savvy thinking was as it was also for the fact that it proved he had managed to get her onboard.

"My cover is safe, Jorja. Artem Sokolov is dead."

CHAPTER THREE

Mixed feelings of grief and gratitude played on her conscience. She'd known and worked with Artem for so long, yet, knowing he would never be able to hurt her, Ben, or anyone else ever again brought her instant relief.

Pascale studied her face and couldn't help notice how the news of Sokolov's death had lifted the tension in Jorja's body and softened the lines on her face, instantly revealing that he might be close to winning her over. Excitement threatened to bubble to the surface, but he kept it at bay. This was the break he'd been praying for. All he needed to do was get Jorja to agree. With nervous tension in his stomach, he broached the burning question. "Do I take it you're on board, then? Will you help me?"

Instinctively, Jorja's eyes turned towards the window, her eyes pinned on the clouds that floated across the morning sky as she said a silent prayer for guidance. Her heart wanted a peaceful existence in St. Ives, free from the criminal past she'd been running from, but her spirit prompted her to accept and trust in God's plan. And as she wrestled back and forth, despite not fully knowing what she'd be agreeing to, in spite of it being the complete opposite of what she so desperately wanted, she found her body yielding to the workings of the Holy Spirit as she turned to face Pascale and nodded in agreement.

When a lonely tear escaped and gently trickled down her cheek, Pascale reached across the table and covered her hand.

"Thank you." His voice was gentle and warm as he said it.

But Jorja pulled her hand away and placed it in her lap instead—she wasn't ready to forgive him yet. Noticing the hint of rejection that flickered in his eyes, she dropped her gaze to the folder in front of him.

Pascale rose to his feet and took the few steps back to the switch on the wall that operated the overhead camera. She had made her feelings about him crystal clear and he was grateful for the opportunity to gather his emotions before he took up his seat at the table again. He flipped open the folder and spread several sheets of paper across the table in front of her. "Recognize these?" His voice was suddenly cool and businesslike.

Jorja didn't need to study them and acknowledged with a slight nod, the space between them suddenly feeling awkward.

"You took these from Franz's safe, at the club."

"I did. What about them?" she asked warily, puzzled with how he even knew that.

"We were hoping you could tell us more about them."

"There's nothing to tell. I was only interested in the folder containing information about the *Salvator Mundi*."

"Yet you decided to keep these hidden in the base of your luggage." Pascale's gaze was penetrating.

Anger welled up inside her and Jorja jumped to her feet and walked away from the table, suddenly feeling as if she was being interrogated rather than being petitioned to help.

Jorja's reaction instantly made Pascale regret his aloof tone. Antagonizing her would only hurt his cause, he thought. Quick to rectify the tension between them, he moved to stand next to her.

"Sorry, occupational hazard," he said with his hands in his pockets as his eyes found hers and his face softened into a handsome smile.

"It's fine," Jorja said, loosely crossing her arms.

"Look, it's been a long couple of days and I am ashamed to admit that I just realized you must be tired and hungry. We can do this another time. I'll get someone to take you to your apartment. I've already taken the liberty of unpacking your luggage and stocking the kitchen with a few essentials."

Jorja's brows furrowed into a curious stare.

"You seem surprised," Pascale responded.

"I am. How did you know I would agree to your terms?"

"I didn't. I just assumed you'd be on the same journey as me to see justice prevail in a broken world. Turns out I was right."

Again he flashed one of his charming smiles.

"Never assume anything, Pascale. Rule number one in this business."

She turned and walked towards her suitcase that still stood to one side and flipped the handle up.

"Oh, it's empty. Like I said, I already had your things placed in your apartment." He spotted the annoyance in Jorja's eyes then quickly continued. "Yes, yes, guilty as charged. You caught me in another one of my interrogation tactics. I apologize." His hand was on his chest.

"I'd appreciate if you refrained from using any more of your devious schemes on me, Pascale. If we're going to work together, I need to know that I can trust you."

His face turned serious. "You're right. No more games and no more lies." He held out his hand to shake on it but she ignored him and headed toward the door, inviting an amused chuckle from her new partner.

"Something tells me I'd better be watching my step with you, Miss Rose, or your thorns might very well draw blood from these fragile hands of mine."

The luxurious, serviced apartment was located in one of the top hotels in Abu Dhabi, not too far from the British Embassy, and Jorja waited until the junior Interpol official that had escorted her there left before she turned to take it all in. Breathtaking views across the glistening Arabian Gulf instantly drew her to the expansive floor-to-ceiling windows on the other end of the room. It was a sight to behold, and she stood there a few moments to capture the mesmerizing beauty of the turquoise waterfront below.

The rest of the open concept apartment incorporated stylish contemporary designs that were complemented by modern regional artwork and traditional accessories. It was spacious yet intimate, warm, and sophisticated all at once, precisely what she would have picked for herself. She walked into the nearby bedroom suite that captured a corner view of the same turquoise scenery and was instantly reminded of the calming seaside views back home. Wondering if she would ever experience the clean crisp sea air on her habitual morning runs along the rugged British coastline, or stroke the soft fur of her darling Vincent again, she turned in search of the shower, eager to wash away the guilt, shame, and hurt that somehow still lingered on her conscience. As the hot water washed away her sadness and the steam soon filled the room, she spilled her heart to the Lord and allowed Him to infuse her with new hope and strength on a journey into the unknown. She asked Him to heal her wounds, to help her forgive Pascale, and to grant her courage for whatever lay ahead.

When she finally slipped between the luxurious Egyptian cotton layers of her bed, swaddled in the plush hotel robe as her damp hair draped across the pillow, her tears dried up.

She had found peace in her situation. Rested in the knowledge that God would not forsake her. That He would keep her foot from slipping as He took her hand and guided her along her path. And, as she prayed, she opened her heart and mind to the notion that, whatever His plan or purpose was for her, it would be fulfilled and that she would be granted the grace and forgiveness to please Him. Soothed into peace as she handed over the reins, she drifted off into a deep sleep.

T he strong aroma of freshly brewed coffee stirred her senses as she slowly woke up. Bright rays beamed through her window and pierced at her eyes as she sat up in bed. She glanced at the digital clock on the bedside table. It was 6:40 a.m. Suddenly realizing that she had slept for nearly eighteen hours, she jumped out of bed and followed the aroma of coffee into the kitchen.

"Ask me how I knew that would do the trick in getting you out of bed." Pascale's voice was suddenly next to her.

"What are you doing here?" she snapped, feeling suddenly aware of being in her bathrobe. She clutched at the collar and tightened the cord.

"Not the reply I was hoping for but I guess perhaps you're not a morning person. In any event, we have business to conclude, remember? Time is of the essence so might I suggest you throw on some clothes while I pour you a mug of the best coffee you've ever tasted. We have a lot to get through."

Pascale's unexpected presence had Jorja's cheeks flush hot and bright red and she quickly disappeared into the bedroom where she found the entire contents of her bag along with several new pieces of clothing in the closet. Why was he having such an effect on her? He was nothing but obnoxious and entirely full of himself. She wriggled her shoulders as if to shake her mind and body back to where she was once again in control of her emotions. Vowing to not let him catch her off guard like that again, she dressed and returned to find him gone, and in his stead, a place was set for her at the dining table where he had fresh coffee and a plate of berry-dressed pancakes waiting for her.

CHAPTER FOUR

The unexpected urgent invitation to meet Gerard Dubois had Pascale feeling more than a little uneasy. Their regular appointed check-in time wasn't for another three days and it was rarely, if ever, that Gerard extended an impromptu request to meet up outside of their usual time—no less an urgent one. But what really had Pascale on edge was the fact that Gerard had traveled to the Emirates to meet him in person instead of meeting him at the *Gardiens* headquarters in Geneva, as was usually the case.

Taking a deep breath to try to settle his nerves, Pascale exited at the rear of Jorja's apartment building—an added precaution just in the event Gerard had uncovered his true identity. Keeping Jorja's involvement hidden for now was of vital importance—for her safety and that of the mission.

Resolving that he'd do whatever he could to maintain his cover, he had left her a note to meet his driver in the lobby after breakfast, after which he had instructed the rest of the team to gather in the Abu Dhabi nerve center where he would catch up with them after he finished with Gerard.

While Pascale drove the short distance to the helipad, where he had arranged for a helicopter to take him to where he was to meet Gerard in Dubai, the events of the past few days swirled in his mind. He was restless, unable to shake the worry that nagged in the back of his mind. He had been extra careful not to leave any trail that could compromise his cover. Was it possible that he might have missed something? Was Jorja right? Did Sokolov manage to get word out before he died?

There was no way to be sure. All he could do now was be alert. More so since he decided to come unarmed, something he now wondered if he'd come to regret. When he stepped into the private helicopter and settled in for the short flight, he inhaled a slow, deep breath as he asked God to keep him safe. A few more steady breaths calmed his spirit and he was once again reminded that he would have never made it this far without his faith. God had been taking care of him and he had no reason to doubt He wouldn't do it again.

The flight went quickly and he soon reached the desolate patch of land on the outskirts of Dubai where he then got into the rental car that had been left for him. But, as he punched the address into his phone's GPS and followed the directions to where he was told to meet Gerard, nerves took hold of him again. His stomach was as tense as the knots in his shoulders and the sick feeling in his stomach increased with every passing second. Being unprepared wasn't how he liked to go to these meetings and he somehow sensed the contents of Franz's files had more to do with this than he was aware. It was entirely possible that Franz had, by now, discovered them stolen and if Gerard was in some way involved in something else behind his back, this meeting might very well hold more risk than he would like. If only he knew what the documents said. Perhaps that would have provided a clue as to what Gerard had up his sleeve and he wouldn't have been so anxious. But even though he had spent most of the past forty-eight hours analyzing the documents alongside his team, no one had been able to decipher the pieces of text.

When he reached the address and pulled up to the large gate, the two surveillance cameras on the wall on either side of it whirred as they focused in on him before a voice came over the intercom next to his window.

"Pascale Lupin to see Mr. Gerard Dubois," he announced in response and waited as the gate promptly opened.

He approached the stately house by a long drive that wound through unexpected lush lawns and palm trees.

Unlike the typical homes found in the Emirates, there were distinct architectural features that resembled a luxurious Spanish hacienda instead of the usual modern architecture one would expect to see in Dubai. It left him feeling even more unnerved. None of it added up to Gerard's personality, so it left him wondering whose house it was.

When he stopped in front of the entrance, he was instantly greeted by two burly men, each armed with an automatic rifle that was draped over one shoulder. Quick to have him get out of the car, one of the men vigorously patted down Pascale's body while the other one followed suit with a handheld scanner. When they were satisfied Pascale wasn't carrying a weapon, they pointed him toward the front door where a pretty young woman invited him inside. He followed her through the stately house to where she ushered him out onto a large shaded poolside terrace where he found Gerard in conversation with a man he had never seen or met.

"There he is! Pascale, come meet my associate, Diego Cortez," Gerard said jovially as he eagerly jumped to his feet, his cigar pinched between his beefy fingers.

"It's a pleasure to meet you," Pascale responded and shook the man's hand. Much to his surprise, the man was neither European nor Arabic.

"So you're the one who found the *Salvator Mundi*," Diego responded, his voice tainted with misguided pride. "I hear it took some doing. Please, sit." The host stretched his palm towards a nearby chair and beckoned to another pretty young girl to pour Pascale a glass of whiskey.

"News travels fast," Pascale said as she handed him the drink.

"When it's of this nature you had better believe it." Diego took off his black aviator glasses and tossed them on the glass table between them.

"You're not from here," Pascale commented when Diego's Spanish accent and strong facial features were undeniably pointing to him being South American.

"My line of work takes me many places, Mr. Lupin. Now, let's get down to business, shall we?"

Struck by how efficiently Diego avoided answering his question, Pascale couldn't help notice the instantaneous change in Gerard's posture and how he had suddenly tensed up. It was a side of him Pascale had never seen before and it instantly put him on high alert. Could it be that Diego was the one pulling all his strings? Could this man be the head of the *Gardiens*?

"I wasn't aware we had business to discuss," Pascale replied and caught the stern glance Diego cast at Gerard who looked increasingly uncomfortable and on edge.

"I haven't had a chance to brief him yet. It all happened so fast," Gerard quickly defended, again shifting uncomfortably in his chair.

"How much?" Diego's voice broke through the awkwardness.

Pascale shot a querying glance at Gerard.

"You've lost me. How much for what?"

Diego dragged back on his cigar then ran a thick, suntanned hand through his greased-back raven hair as he stared out across the pool in front of them.

From the corner of his eye Pascale noticed Gerard's discomfort when he nervously threw back his whiskey. What was it about Diego that made Gerard act so nervous and inferior? The man, though somewhat authoritative, was nearly half his age.

"Let's not waste time with silly games, Mr. Lupin."

"I couldn't agree more, Mr. Cortez, but I'm afraid I have no idea what you are referring to. Unless you're talking about the *Salvator Mundi*, in which case I am afraid to say it isn't up for sale. I'm sure Gerard would agree." Pascale looked to Gerard to back him up but he refrained from doing so.

"I'm not interested in buying the *Salvator Mundi*, Mr. Lupin. I'm interested in you."

Pascale felt a lump form in his throat. Whatever this man was going to offer could jeopardize his entire mission.

"I'm listening," he forced a reply, suddenly not feeling half as confident as he let on.

"I need your help with a small business matter."

Pascale shot Gerard an inquiring look. Unsurprisingly, he was still keeping to himself.

"My help with what, exactly? I'm sure Gerard already filled you in on what I do for the *Gardiens*, so, with respect, I'm not sure I understand how I could be of service to you."

Diego killed his cigar in the crystal ashtray next to him, using more force than Pascale cared to see. When he turned to face Pascale, his eyes were dark and the pock-marks on his face, which suddenly appeared deeper, made him seem even more intimidating than before.

Diego clasped his hands on top of the table and leaned in. "Did you not just steal one of the world's most famous paintings that the entire universe believed was lost forever, Mr. Lupin? And, as I understand it, you managed to penetrate one of the tightest security initiatives I've ever seen in order to do it. So, which part of 'I want to hire you' don't you understand?"

Pascale placed his untouched drink on the table, the air between them suddenly feeling dangerously strained.

"I'm flattered, but with respect, Mr. Cortez, I'm not a thief. This was a one-time gig."

Gerard nearly choked when Pascale's answer caught him in the middle of taking another swig of his drink and he intervened for the first time.

"You're not here to refuse Diego's offer, Pascale. You'll do as he says." He turned his attention to Diego. "He will agree to whatever you need him to do. And he will do it at no charge."

Diego smirked. Clearly he was a man who didn't need to beg in order to get precisely what he wanted, and Gerard was all too eager to accede to his demands.

"Good, I am glad we agree." He snapped his fingers at one of his security guards who had been standing to one side. The man handed Pascale a disposable flip-phone then promptly resumed his watchful position.

"Keep it on. You'll get a text with more details." Diego stood up and turned to face Pascale. "And I'm sure I don't need to remind you to keep this meeting between us, correct? I am not a man who likes surprises, Mr. Lupin. Gerard speaks highly of you so I am going to choose to take his word for it. Trust is everything in my line of business. Break it, and you won't live to see another day. *Comprende?*"

"Understood," Pascale replied, before Diego turned and disappeared inside his house.

CHAPTER FIVE

Pascale turned to face Gerard as soon as Diego was out of sight, his fists and jaw clenched as he struggled to contain the fury that raged inside him. "Care to tell me what just happened here, Gerard? You just offered me up to this man like a sacrificial lamb, forced to participate in whatever his *line of business* might be. I have been working for you for a very long time and I think I deserve an explanation on what you just got me involved with."

Gerard downed the rest of his liquor, his confidence suddenly back in its usual form as he closed the space between them. His face was red with anger and his words harsh. When he spoke, his thin lips suddenly white, drops of excess liquor splattered into Pascale's face.

"Let's not forget that you answer to me, Lupin, and that means you do whatever I tell you because that's what you are paid to do. And if your duties extend to one of my associates, you comply and keep your mouth shut. You were only here because he insisted on meeting you. Do as he says and you will walk away alive. Got it?" When Gerard noisily set the empty glass down on the table and pushed past Pascale, there was nothing more to say.

Like it or not, Pascale was in Gerard's employ and, unless he wanted to blow his entire operation, he had no choice but to do as Gerard Dubois saw fit—even if it meant his life and cover were at stake.

The two men parted ways without saying another word. But it was clear by the worried look on Gerard's face and his standoffish demeanor that he too had a lot on his mind. His mood was dark, almost brooding, and if Pascale didn't know him better, he could have sworn Gerard was angry as well.

As Pascale made the solo trip back to Abu Dhabi, the questions in his mind came hard and fast. Why did it seem that Gerard wasn't pleased with the outcome of the meeting? And if he wasn't happy about what transpired, why was he so eager to please Diego in the first place? Was he being blackmailed? More importantly, what were Diego and Gerard wanting him to do?

. . .

W hen Pascale walked into the nerve center nearly two hours later, his team—and Jorja —were already waiting for him. The pensive look on his face instantly told them something was amiss.

"Everything okay, boss?" It was Kalihm who spoke first the moment Pascale tossed his navy blazer over the sofa.

But Pascale ignored the question as he rolled up his white sleeves and called his cyber agent to attention. "Harry, I need you to pull up everything you can find on a Diego Cortez. Spanish, possibly Columbian, mid-thirties. Airlock your search—I need to keep this under wraps for now. And I need it yesterday, please."

"On it, boss," the young intelligence member complied and immediately set about on his keyboard.

"What's going on?" Jorja asked. "Who's this Cortez guy?"

"That's what I'm planning on finding out. Any progress on Franz's files?"

"Nothing yet. It's a bunch of words and weird looking pictures that I can't make heads or tails out of. We've been at it non-stop."

"Well, we're going to need to try harder. If we are to make any progress in taking down the *Gardiens*, we need to find out who's at the top." He moved over to where the contents of the folders lay scattered on the table and started poring over it. "And, Kalihm, run another background check on Sokolov's team. Make sure we didn't miss anything."

"Copy that," Kalihm replied and jumped right into the task.

Sensing to leave him be, Jorja kept working on the files without prodding him with more questions.

"You're not going to like this, boss," Harry announced a short while later as he sent his findings to the large computer screen on the wall.

Pascale took up position in front of the screen with the rest of the team behind him as Harry continued.

"Diego Juan Cortez. Thirty-four and linked to the Moreno cartel. Columbia's biggest cocaine manufacturers, for those who don't know who they are." He smirked. "Anyway, he has several priors ranging from auto theft to weapons trade but the most significant is, of course, illegal distribution of narcotics. Yet, the man's never been convicted. I found several classified files, some of them sealed by the FBI. Don't worry, I managed to get in, but be prepared to have your minds blown with what I found inside." Harry paused for effect that quickly got him a raised eyebrow from Pascale in return. "Fine, I won't keep you in suspense. It seems he has quite a few Supreme Court judges in his pocket and, just in case that's not enough leverage, a bunch of dirty politicians too. So, for the sake of politics, the man's essentially untouchable. It is my calculated assumption that these crooked judges and politicians either turn a blind eye because they're clients, or because they're being paid to look the other way. Either way, they've been cleaning up after this guy, big time."

Pascale's hands folded into fists where he stood staring at the face of the man he had just met. A million questions raced through his mind as a combination of fear and anger took hold. He knew Gerard's influence stretched to a few of these crimes, but never narcotics. So why was he in business with one of the world's biggest drug cartels? And what was it that Gerard just forced him into?

He turned away from the screen and paced the room, his hand vigorously rubbing at a headache that had shown up across his forehead.

"Boss, are you in some kind of trouble?" Mo asked. "Who is this guy and what's he got to do with the *Gardiens*?" His question caught the amused attention of both Harry and Kalihm since, usually, Mo only showed an interest in speaking when it was time to bring out the ammunition.

"What? It's my job to make sure our weapons can handle this guy," he justified his actions against their curious stares.

Jorja, who had been quietly observing, could also no longer hold back. "Pascale, what's going on? Why are you looking into this guy?"

Pascale's hands went to his hips as his gaze returned to Diego's picture on the screen. "Because my meeting with Gerard included this guy in his house in Dubai and Gerard strong-armed me into doing some kind of job for him."

Stunned to silence, the team tried to process the information.

"Yes, I know, this could potentially blow our entire operation out of the water," Pascale exploded.

"Do you think he's after the *Salvator Mundi*?" Jorja asked.

"Apparently not. I asked. I was given a burner phone and told to wait for instructions. Oh, and to keep my mouth shut."

"And Gerard was on board with this?" Kalihm asked.

"And some! The guy pulled rank on me. What's more, is that he was like a timid little puppy in Cortez's company. As if he was too afraid to say no to the man."

"Or perhaps Cortez is his superior," Mo guessed.

"I thought of that too but Gerard referred to Cortez as his associate."

"Do you think your cover is blown?" Jorja asked.

"No, it's solid. This is about something else."

"Something other than taking ownership of a priceless piece of art?" she queried, to which Pascale nodded.

"Well, if it's not about the painting then what else would he want to use you for?" Mo said, looking as puzzled as the rest of them.

Pascale turned his focus back to his team. "I have no idea, but whatever it is, Gerard is involved too. And if Gerard is working for this guy, the entire *Gardiens* is connected to him."

Pascale returned to the files on the table. "One way or another, regardless of where Cortez fits into the picture right now, we can't lose sight of our mission. Our primary focus remains on getting to the head of the snake and taking down the *Gardiens*. Whatever Gerard roped himself—and me—into, I'll have to handle separately. And that only leaves me to do one thing. I need to pay our dear friend, Franz, a little visit—check in and see if he lets something slip. And while I keep him occupied," he looked at Jorja, "you have to return these files to his office."

CHAPTER SIX

"Return them? Why would we do that? Isn't the entire point of holding onto them to figure out what's written on these sheets of paper?" Jorja said looking perplexed.

"It is, and we will make copies and continue working on them. But since we haven't made any headway, and time is of the essence, we follow the breadcrumbs and hope it leads us to where we need to go."

Harry cheered from behind his screen. "Brilliant plan, Boss. I'll get them to fuel up the jet!"

"Will someone fill me in please because I have no idea what's going here. If you need help with blowing open the safe, I'm your man." Mo said.

"We're not blowing anything up just yet, Mo. We're going to give Franz his files back so we can hopefully trace his steps to see what he's up to," Jorja explained.

"Exactly," Pascale confirmed as the corners of his lips curled into a slight smile that very nearly brought Jorja's guard down. But she held back, made sure not to let his charm deceive her again. Pascale Lupin was loyal only to his mission—to take down the *Gardiens*.

She had entered into a plea to free Ben and to pay her dues, her penance for all the crimes she'd committed. She didn't need to trust Pascale. She shouldn't. All she needed was to see it through. And once her debts were finally paid, she'd walk away from it all. For good.

With a plan in motion to set the course, Pascale and Jorja's minds occupied by far more than what was on the table between them, Kalihm broke the silence.

"Boss, I forgot to tell you. I took care of the *Salvator Mundi* as requested. The delivery to the *Gardiens* headquarters went off without a hitch."

"That's great to hear, Kalihm. Thank you," Pascale replied.

The surprising information punched Jorja in her gut, leaving her face hot with mounting rage that she had to fight to hold back.

"What do you mean you had it delivered to the *Gardiens*?" Her voice was low and restrained as she battled to control her anger. The thought of once again losing the painting to the criminal underworld ripped at her heart. "Please, tell me you didn't hand a priceless piece of art back into the hands of Europe's largest crime syndicate? Have you lost your mind?"

Pascale studied Jorja's face. She was visibly upset, her passion for the craft clearly noticeable and it reminded Pascale of their conversations on the plane. It was that very quality in her that had instantly bonded them. Except this time, there was something far worse than betrayal hidden in her eyes, veiled by the words she spoke. It was in the way she looked at him, the way her eyes burned into his, and the way it stabbed at his heart. She hated him.

And as is often the case when internal walls go up, Pascale pushed back.

"You didn't think I was actually going to hand it over to Sokolov, did you?"

"No, but I also didn't think you would give it to Gerard! It was all just another one of your lies. You were never going to return the painting to the Bouvier Foundation. You wanted it for yourself, to serve your selfish obsession with taking down the *Gardiens*. It's all you care about. I knew you couldn't be trusted. I should have never trusted a man like you!" She screamed the words at him as she bolted out the door.

Jorja's words sliced into Pascale's soul. She hated him more now than ever before. Unable to let it go, he turned and ran after her. When he caught up with her and stopped her at the end of the corridor, sarcasm laced his words.

"I did what I had to do, Jorja. It's my job. I'm sorry if being on the right side of the law taking criminals like you down for good doesn't sit well with you. You got what you wanted, Jorja. More than you needed! Ben's life was saved *and* he received his freedom. I kept my side of the deal. Can you keep yours? Besides, I couldn't very well tell you that I had also promised the painting to Gerard, could I? I have a job to do, Jorja. One that serves the right side of the law. Sokolov was a welcomed bonus, the sweet cherry on the top, a means to an end, and the way I see it, so are you."

Jorja's eyes instantly filled with tears as Pascale's stabbing words pierced her unprepared heart. Too hurt to sling back, the words caught in her throat and she pinned her eyes on his. Staring deep into his soul, unable to hide just how much his words had hurt her, tears tumbled freely down onto her cheeks.

Pascale buried his face in his hands, instantly regretting the jarring words he had thrust at her before he took the few steps toward her. Closing the space between them, his eyes now filled with regret, he tried getting her to look at him. But, Jorja looked away, crossing her arms firmly as if to shield her broken heart. She had already shut him out, and there was no turning back.

Desperate to recant his words, deeply regretting his lack of self-control, Pascale pleaded with her.

"I'm sorry, Jorja, I didn't mean what I said." His voice was filled with regret and shame as he continued. "Sometimes I forget who I am. At least, the person I used to be. I am so desperately trying not to lose myself in all of this. It's been a while—playing two sides of the game, and sometimes the lines get blurred. It's no excuse, I know. I shouldn't have said what I did. I didn't mean it. You have every right to be angry with me. I get it. I'd hate me too. I'm truly sorry for lying to you, but I couldn't let you in back then. I didn't know who you were. But things are different now. I realize I'm asking a lot, but please, trust me. I know what I'm doing. I promise I'll make it up to you." He moved even closer and placed his hands on her elbows. "Gerard doesn't have the painting, nor would he ever get his grubby little hands on it. I gave him a replica—he'll never know the difference. Authenticating his art is, after all, one of the many jobs he pays me to do. The original painting is safe, and as it stands, you and I are the only two people who know this. Not even my team knows, and I'd like to keep it that way."

When Jorja offered no lifeline, he continued. "Look, it's not like I had a choice. I don't like this any more than you do, but you know as well as I do that the second we reveal that painting to the world all of this goes up in a cloud of smoke. Gerard thinks he has the real thing and it needs to stay that way or he'll know I double-crossed him. I can't risk it. You're not the only one who gave up the people you loved. I've given up everything to become someone I'm not. I have just as much riding on this as you." His voice broke with emotion as he blurted out the final two sentences. "I promise, the moment all of this is over, I will make sure the *Salvator Mundi* gets all the honor it deserves. I give you my word. I don't believe it was a coincidence that I found you that night in the church, Jorja, and I'll even venture so far as to say that I know God's hand was in it. So, even if I don't know if you have met God, I trust Him, and I trust that you crossed my path for a reason. Even if I don't yet know what that reason is."

Jorja looked into Pascale's eyes for the first time. As he revealed his faith she felt her heart softening, reconsidered her anger toward him and the situation and forgiveness suddenly tugged at her heart. The very faith he spoke of she shared, and in the very God he trusted, she trusted also.

Staring into Pascale's eyes, her attention anchored on every sincere word he spoke, her heart and thoughts mesmerized by his magnetic presence, Jorja found herself yielding. Something in his eyes had given her assurance, given her peace, told her to let him in, to trust him—to trust God. And as the tension in her body slowly melted away and she was reminded of God's love, she found her heart softening and her walls crumbling down. Whatever the journey ahead may bring, she was safe with him. For Pascale Lupin was in a battle of his own, fighting the same demons she was, protected by the God they both served. Perhaps they had more in common than she cared to admit. Perhaps the very reason their paths had crossed was not to bring down enemies, but because they needed one another to each find their way to a place of peace.

And as Jorja allowed her heart to be softened and forgiveness to settle in, she allowed him back in and whispered, "I trust you because I trust God."

Where they stood at the end of the corridor, each choosing to believe their faith had brought them together, they surrendered to God's plan.

But before the moment had the chance to become more, Harry's voice echoed down the hallway.

"Boss! We have a message on the burner!"

CHAPTER SEVEN

The burner phone traveled through the air as Harry tossed it to Pascale, who flipped it open the instant he caught it.

Details of a place and time flashed across the small screen, instantly filling Pascale with dread. He slammed the flip phone's body back in place.

"What did it say?" Jorja prompted when she noticed the tightening of the muscles in his jaw.

"Not much, just instructions to be at a specified address at eleven tonight." He rubbed at the back of his neck as they returned to the nerve center and handed the phone back to Harry. "Find out everything you can on the address he sent through."

Pascale turned to scan the contents on the large screen again. "I don't like this. Why is Gerard involved with this guy? There has to be something we missed." His angst was instantly evident to the rest of the team.

"Do you think it's a trap?" Kalihm asked. "What if Gerard found out that you are Interpol and this is an ambush?"

Pascale shook his head. "I don't think so. I would've seen it in his face. He was scared of Diego. Too scared to say no to whatever it is this man wants me to do."

"I'm going with you," Jorja said.

"No, it's too dangerous. Diego made it very clear not to involve anyone else."

"Except, if it does have something to do with the *Salvator Mundi*, you don't really have much of a choice since you weren't the one who stole the painting. I did. So, if he's planning on having you steal another one, isn't it best he knows you had a partner? Besides, there's strength in numbers." Jorja said as her lips curled into a slight smile.

"Are you sure you can handle this? I have no idea what to expect and these guys aren't exactly your average criminals. These are dangerous people, Jorja."

She nodded. "I'm sure. We're in this together, remember?"

Pascale's eyes lit up. Knowing that they had each other's backs made all the difference. Besides, he could do with the back-up and she was skilled enough to handle anything that came her way.

"Fine, but you take my lead, got it?"

Jorja saluted playfully.

"All right then," Harry interjected, his voice equally amused and uncomfortable at their sudden flirtatious camaraderie. "I take it we're not heading back to Geneva anymore, so I'll cancel the jet."

"No, don't." Pascale turned to face Kalihm before he continued. "I'm going to need you to return the files to Franz's office since Jorja's with me. I'll send Franz on a wild goose chase and make sure he's not at the club. Harry will bypass the club's security by tapping into his mainframe. Bury the files somewhere on his desk, not too deep though. We want him to take the bait. Better yet, if you have one of those fancy miniature trackers of yours, we'll monitor the folders on top of Franz's movements. I need you to stay on his tail, watch his every move."

"Copy that," Kalihm said.

"What about our rendezvous tonight? Shouldn't we familiarize ourselves with the location? Exit routes, for example." Jorja said, switching gears.

"Spoken like a pro," Mo added. "You'll need my help. With Kalihm gone, I can step in and keep an eye on you, keep you in my sights."

"You'll have to sit out on this one, Mo. I doubt his plan is to kill me. Besides, if they so much as see you I'll lose whatever trust he has in me and right now, I have no choice but to go along with what he's planning."

"Your wish is my command, boss," Mo replied.

"What do we know about the location?" Jorja asked.

"It's in an abandoned building on the outskirts of town," Harry reported. "As far as I know it's been empty for years. It used to be an old shipping warehouse before the larger courier companies moved into the country. I'm trying to locate any nearby surveillance cameras, but so far my search has turned up empty. There's nothing around within a two-mile radius. It's too far out of the city."

"What about the ownership of the land?" Pascale asked.

"I'm still looking into it. All I found so far is that it's registered to a shell company. And someone went through a lot of trouble to conceal the names of its members."

Pascale glanced at his watch then moved to where Diego's background check was still on display on the large computer screen. As he studied the details again, his body tensed.

"Have you managed to dig up anything new on Diego?" he asked Harry.

"Negative, boss."

"Well, then we have no choice but to let it play out and see how far Kalihm gets. Franz is bound to slip up somewhere."

T he meeting time drew closer faster than Jorja and Pascale would have liked, but they were as prepared as anyone could be in a situation where they knew next to nothing about who they were up against. As they drove Pascale's car down the orange, sand-blown road, it quickly became clear why Diego Cortez had chosen to meet at that address. Located on the very outskirts of Abu Dhabi's old city, it was nearly entirely surrounded by desert sand. Nerves had settled in both Jorja's and Pascale's stomachs, and as they approached the large locked gate, Pascale shuffled uncomfortably in his seat. As his whitened knuckles pressed firmly on the steering wheel, he took in the full extent of the property.

Tall, barbed wire fences encircled the abandoned storage structure, which was further secured by even taller electric fences.

Along the outer perimeter, watchtowers stood tall at each corner post, armed with watchmen who patrolled every angle of the property. On either side of the gated entrance were two more guard posts, each occupied by at least three armed men. Short of escaping on camelback through the desert, there was only one way in, and it happened to also be the only way out.

"It's starting to look a lot like a high security prison, if you ask me. Makes me wonder if he's planning on locking us up in here," Pascale said as his hands tightened even more around the steering wheel as soon as the first spotlight lit up the area around the car.

"I am very certain he doesn't have people locked up inside here. Take a good look around. There's nothing but desert all around us. No sewerage hatches, no evidence of water tanks, nothing that would be essential to keep anything alive inside there for extended periods of time. The electricity runs off a solar grid, and then there're those, over there." Jorja pushed her chin out towards a small fleet of vehicles parked to one side.

Pascale's eyes lingered on them. "Custom transport vans, like the ones used by the museums."

"Yep, moisture controlled and specifically adapted to transport valuable works of art."

They shared a brief triumphant smile as Pascale pulled up to the gate and slowly let his window down.

Two guards rushed towards Jorja and Pascale, momentarily blinding them as the guards blasted their bright flashlights into their eyes. Flanking the car, they then signaled for Pascale to roll down Jorja's window. He did so without hesitation and the guards quickly shoved the barrels of their rifles through the window openings.

"Hands on the dash!" one commanded, which Pascale and Jorja quickly adhered to.

Moments later, one of the guards spoke Spanish into a two-way radio while their guns still held Jorja and Pascale captive.

"He's asking about me," Jorja whispered from the side of her mouth so as to not attract the guards' attention.

"You speak Spanish?" Pascale whispered back.

"Some."

"No speaking!" the guard hushed them, shoving his gun's barrel right up against Jorja's cheek.

When a voice on the radio came back, the guard yanked Pascale's door open and threw him over the hood on his side of the car.

"Who's the woman?" the guard demanded.

"My partner, she's cool."

"Señor Cortez wants a name!" the guard pushed the tip of his gun deeper into the muscly flesh between Pascale's shoulder blades.

"Jorja...Rose," he groaned as the stabbing pain momentarily caused him to lose his breath.

The guard promptly relayed her name through the radio and waited for a reply. Almost instantly he got what he needed and shouted a command to the other guard who was quick to follow his orders.

He too yanked Jorja from the car and shoved her against the front of the car where he forced her face-first down onto the hood opposite Pascale. She let out a soft groan when the edge of the car knocked her wind out.

"Take it easy!" Pascale shouted as his eyes locked with Jorja's to check if she was okay. But her face was held down on the hood as the guard heavy-handedly searched her clothing for weapons. Pascale and Jorja had preempted a body-search and was relieved their foresight had paid off. Moments later, the guards covered their eyes with black blindfolds, then bound their hands behind their backs.

As the guards shoved them to get walking, Jorja tripped and fell forward, planting face-first in the dirt.

CHAPTER EIGHT

Jorja's captor pulled her to her feet and firmed his grip around her arm as he pressed his body closer into her back.

The putrid smell of old sweat and stale cigarette smoke filled her nostrils and she instinctively buried her nose into her opposite shoulder. Assuming she was trying to get the blindfold off, the man swore at her, then jerked her to a halt. Rough hands closed over her eyes as he checked that the blindfold was still in place.

"You look again, I'll leave you in the trunk of the car," he warned.

Knowing he meant it, even if she wasn't guilty of his accusation, Jorja made sure she stayed in step with him, focusing her remaining senses on tracking her surroundings instead.

Although she couldn't see him, she knew Pascale was in front of her by the way his feet dragged noisily through the sandy soil beneath them. It was his way of letting her know he was close by, she thought.

A few turns followed before they were told to stop, then a door buzzed open somewhere to their right. Heavy hands shoved them through the doorway, where once inside, a wave of hot air right away hit against their faces.

Instantly, disappointment washed over Jorja as she realized she was wrong to assume the storage facility might hold any works of art. It was far too hot inside the building for art to be preserved. In an attempt to have more time to blindly sense her surrounds, she tried to slow her pace, but her keeper shoved her forward, uttering a stream of native oaths in the process.

"Jorja, are you okay?" Pascale chanced speaking.

"No talking!" his keeper yelled when Pascale overstepped.

"Where are you taking us?" Jorja asked the guard, cleverly masking a reply to Pascale.

"Just walk!"

They must have misjudged the size of the facility because it took some distance and several more turns before they stopped again. The now distinct sound of an electronic lock buzzing open another door filled the hot space and they were soon ushered down a flight of steel stairs—evident by the way their footsteps echoed under their feet. As they reached the bottom of the stairs, the air instantly turned cooler. They were underground.

A few more steps and another door buzzed open in front of them. This time though, the guards didn't walk through the doorway with them. Instead, they pulled off their blindfolds, freed their hands, then nudged them inside the other room. As the pair stumbled forward, the guards shut the door behind them, leaving Jorja and Pascale on their own inside the semi-lit underground space.

Expecting to have been apprehended to a dungeon, Jorja and Pascale found themselves frozen in place instead, their eyes wide and their mouths open as they took in the space around them. Stretching out in front of them, was a spacious room that bore a striking resemblance to a small exhibition hall in a museum. Rich tones of burgundy and beige covered the walls, setting a warm and cozy ambience. But it was what adorned the walls that captivated the pair's attention. At a loss for words, where they now stood in awe in the center of the large room, rows of paintings surrounded them. There were works by Rembrandt, Van Gogh, Monet, Cézanne, Da Vinci, and Degas. All of which had been stolen at one time or another in the past. Stunned they took it all in until Diego's voice suddenly echoed through the silence.

"I thought you might appreciate my little collection," he said, suddenly next to them.

Looking as smug and authoritative as he did when Pascale had first met him, he was dressed in an expensive off-white suit he wore over a black collared shirt with matching shiny black loafers. A single gold chain peeked out from behind his half-unbuttoned shirt which matched the pure gold cufflinks that carried his initials. A few paces behind him, two black-suited bodyguards stood watch, their hands neatly folded in front of them as if they were protecting a president.

"So, what do you think? Impressive, right?" he continued as he glanced around the room with pride. But when neither Jorja or Pascale offered any response, his attention turned to Jorja instead.

"Yes, I know, it's a lot to take in. But perhaps I should be the one who's in shock. Imagine my surprise when I heard I was going to be lucky enough to finally meet *the* Jorja Rose." He clicked his tongue in quick succession while he looked her up and down.

"I don't believe we've met," Jorja said.

"Indeed we haven't, at least not in the flesh. But, in a roundabout way, we have actually been associates for decades." Diego smirked mysteriously, his comment inviting curious stares from both his guests.

"The look on your faces is priceless. But be careful. I'm feeling a bit judged by you two right now. We're birds of the same feathers, really. Career criminals bound by repu-tation. And in our line of business, everyone's paths cross sooner or later, whether you choose it to or not. But I'm sure you know all about that already don't you, Jorja? Your reputation precedes you. At least the one linked to your real name."

The information sent shockwaves through Jorja's body but she held firm to her poker face.

"You clearly know a lot more about me than I do about you. Why is that?" Jorja asked boldly.

Diego leaned in, his dark eyes sending chills down her spine as they fixed on hers.

"You really don't know, do you?" he grinned. "Allow me to fill you in then. We had a mutual acquaintance. Actually, he and I were more than acquaintances. We were business partners, *compadres*. Or so I foolishly thought. The guy sure did me dirty. Lucky for him, though, he met his demise before I had the satisfaction of ripping his treacherous heart out. And, as I understand it, you had the plea-sure of watching him die. I'll admit, I was a bit envious when I heard someone else got to him first."

Jorja's breath caught in her throat as she instantly realized who Diego spoke of.

"And there it is, written all over your pretty face. You just figured it out, didn't you?"

Jorja nodded. "Yes, I was there. But, I can't understand why Gustav Züber's death brings you so much joy if moments ago you said he was your business partner."

Diego took a step back and turned to face Pascale. "Which, leads to precisely the reason I brought you here." He paused, his face suddenly dark as he studied the concerned look on Pascale's face. "I would have preferred it if you were a bit more forthcoming about your involvement with Jorja. You should have told me you weren't the one who stole the *Salvator Mundi*. Unless you were hiding that piece of information from Gerard, of course." His eyes narrowed, as if he knew a secret.

But Pascale was quick with an answer. "Had I known at the time that your interest in me was art related, I would have happily volunteered the information."

"Yet, here she is. Clearly you had the sense to bring her along. And why is that, Pascale? Did you do a bit of poking around on me, realized that she might come in handy?"

"I wouldn't be doing my job if I didn't. Gerard employs me for protecting his assets. I know art and I'm the best at what I do. It was simply a matter of prediction," Pascale answered, desperate to maintain his front.

"Well, then let's get down to business, shall we?" he turned on his heels, placed his hands behind his back and walked over to admire one of the Rembrandt paintings.

"Gustav Züber chose to make an enemy of me when he stabbed me in the back. The weasel crossed the line when he got his grubby little paws on one of my consignments and then sold my paintings to several private collectors all over the world. But of course, the backstabbing worm got himself killed before I could get any information out of him. Be that as it may, I too am good at what I do, and I do know, since he managed to steal from me while he was behind bars, he had to have worked with someone on the outside. That individual's identity, is yet unknown to me." He scoffed as he looked over his shoulder to Jorja. "For all I know, it might even have been you." His eyes bore through Jorja's before he turned his gaze back to the Rembrandt in front of him, then continued. "But, since I now know you're the one who blew the whistle on him in the first place, hiding on the other side of the world yourself, I think it is safe to assume that it wasn't you." Diego turned around and faced them, his hands still clasped behind his back. "Lucky for me, I got most of my paintings back but three of my paintings are still unaccounted for and I need the pair of you to find them and bring them back to me."

"I don't see how we can help you. It's impossible. Those paintings could be anywhere," Pascale said.

Diego's chin jutted out while his eyebrows lowered into a stern expression as he glared at Pascale. "Didn't you just tell me that you were the best? Not to mention that you will now have the added bonus of having Jorja help you. As I see it, it will be a brisk walk in the park for the two of you. Besides, neither of you have much choice in the matter. You, Pascale, work for the *Gardiens* and they definitely can't afford to lose my business. In a way, I pay your salary." He turned to Jorja. "And as for you, I figure you owe me since someone has to pay for what Züber did to me. And since he's already dead, your association with him makes you the closest match to taking his place. Your skills are unsurpassed, which means you should get the job done in half the time. You've heard the expression 'time is money', and time is something I don't have." He smirked before he ended the conversation by bluntly saying, "Everything I know about the paintings is in an envelope you'll find in your car. I suggest you put your brilliant minds together and get cracking. I'm not a very patient man and neither are my clients. And before I forget, don't bother sharing this location with any of your *friends*. This is just a halfway stop. These precious works of art won't be here by the time the sun rises."

He turned to leave the room and Jorja called after him.

"And what makes you think we'll go along with this?"

Diego paused mid stride then turned to face them. "Because you both want something you haven't been able to accomplish on your own and I'm the only one who can make those dreams a reality."

Then, as quickly as he stepped into the room, he turned and disappeared behind a door neither of them had noticed before.

CHAPTER NINE

It was well past midnight when Diego's henchmen delivered them back to the car, and as soon as their blindfolds were removed, Pascale jumped into the car in search of the envelope. As promised, the small manilla envelope lay in the console between the two front seats. Its contents? A memory stick.

He quickly slipped the flash drive back into the envelope and buried the package inside his blazer's pocket.

"What just happened back there?" Jorja asked as she snapped her seatbelt in place and settled into her seat.

"I'm still trying to digest it myself. I mean, I knew this guy had powerful people in his pocket but one thing's for sure, he must know I'm an Interpol agent." Pascale hastily swung the car around, kicking clouds of sand up behind it as they sped off.

"I hate to say it, Pascale, but I think you might be right. Although it makes no sense why he wouldn't just kill you. Unless it benefits him more in some way, of course. Or we could simply be assuming wrong. But if he does know who you are then it's pretty obvious someone in your department is on Diego's payroll. Someone high enough in rank to have access to classified information. What are you going to do?"

Pascale stared blankly out into the dark road in front of them, the reality of the situation punching hard at his stomach.

"Right now, I have no idea. But what I do know, is if we don't get those paintings, I have no doubt in my mind that Diego will rat me out to Gerard and then nearly ten years of my life and work will be washed down the drain. Not to mention that I'll probably end up dead." Pascale scoffed. "It all makes sense though. For years I've come so close to taking them down. Close enough that I would literally be one step away from arresting the man. But each time I think this is it, Gerard ends up being one step ahead of me and I'm right back where I started. Every single time. So, I guess I'll have to do what Diego says and hope he delivers on his obscured promise. Besides, he's right. It's not like I have any other choice. If I don't go along with it, this case will go up in smoke. What's worse is that you and Ben will go down with it. The deal is only as good as the success of this case. And clearly someone wants me to fail."

Jorja's breath caught in her throat. "And Ben and I will spend the rest of our lives behind bars."

Pascale nodded, unable to look at her and see the disappointment in her eyes. "The only thing I can do is stick with the original plan, now more than ever. I need to bring these guys down, once and for all."

For the rest of the way to Jorja's temporary apartment, they drove in silence—neither wanting to expound on the perilous predicament they were in and both needing the silence to process what had happened. By the time they entered her apartment, it was evident from the deep frown lines etched into Pascale's forehead, that the dire situation he now found himself in weighed heavily on his mind.

But Jorja had been doing a fair bit of grappling on her own and her silence caused Pascale to finally say something.

"You okay?" he asked with care.

She nodded as she chewed her bottom lip without answering him.

"Okay, out with it. What are you thinking?"

She smiled. "Is it that obvious?"

"Only if a bleeding lip isn't anything to go by, no, not really." His eyes twinkled as he said it and she giggled in response.

"Bad habits die hard." She blotted the tiny drop of blood with the back of her hand.

"So, are you going to make me beg? Tell me what's going on in that beautiful head of yours."

She blushed and turned away before she answered him. "I can't seem to wrap my head around why these three particular paintings hold such great value to Diego that he's prepared to pull out all the stops."

"I'm not following you. If they are highly priced paintings, which judging from his collection they'd have to be, then there's hardly anything weird about it."

"Well, think about it. The guy knows you're an Interpol agent, working undercover to take down the *Gardiens*. An organization which, in his words, can't afford to lose his business."

"Okay, so he has to be one of the *Gardiens'* clients. Not that I've ever met or heard about him before, but then again, clearly Gerard has been holding out on me."

"Yes, he's a client, and I presume, a valuable one. But, judging by the way you said Gerard had acted around him, he's not just any client, is he? Clearly there's something more there."

"Have you met the man? Diego Cortez is intimidating, even to me."

"Sure, but I presume Gerard isn't a pushover either so, why would he be intimidated by Diego and why is Diego prepared to sever that relationship with the *Gardiens* by helping you take them down? Wouldn't he be shooting himself in the foot?"

"I see your point."

Jorja paced the room as she thought through the problem. "Unless," she blurted out, "the paintings are worth far more to him than whatever he gets from his relationship with the *Gardiens*, right? But that's another thing I can't seem to figure out. Did you take a good look at the paintings he had on those walls? They're worth more than enough on their own. Add to that the *Salvator Mundi* I'm assuming Gerard's now going to hand to him on a silver platter, and the man will have more money than he can dream to spend in one lifetime. So why bother with three more? What's so special about them? It can't all be about the money and he certainly didn't strike me as one who pays a particularly keen interest in the art itself."

Pascale fell silent and rubbed at the back of his neck, then cracked it to both sides to release the built-up tension that had settled between the bones.

"It's been a long day and an even longer night. We should get some rest," he said, then moved to stand in front of her. "I'm sorry I got you caught up in all of this. None of this was ever part of my plan. I should've never forced your hand, blackmailed you into working with me."

His voice was loaded with remorse and the despair lay evident in his eyes.

"It's not your fault. Clearly Gustav Züber had a lot of enemies, and somehow the despicable fool still manages to make my life a misery, even from his grave. He was rotten to the core and I'm not sure I'll ever fully be rid of the burdens of my past. As it should be, I guess. No sin goes unpunished, right?" She put up a brave smile then turned toward the small kitchen where she set about making a pot of chamomile tea.

"You can't truly believe that, do you?" said Pascale as he moved closer.

"Why not? Isn't that the point of sin? If you do wrong you have to bear the consequences, pay your dues."

"I suppose that will be the case if you're only looking at it from a human's perspective, but when you see it the way

God does, sin is merely a means to Christ-like transformation. We sin, we repent, we change and thus become more like Christ. In my experience, God doesn't hold your mistakes against you if you are a believer. That's why He sent His Son, to wipe the slate clean. He shows you grace, and where He chooses to withhold His grace, He shows you mercy."

Jorja's eyes lingered on his face as she digested his wisdom. "You seem to know a lot about this. I can't say I pegged you as a believer."

Pascale laughed. "It happened a long time ago. Let's just say I was brought to my knees the hard way. I can't do my job any other way. Besides, I might say the same about you. Jorja Rose, master thief turned saint."

"Saint? I wouldn't go that far. I'm still fairly new at this."

"Then perhaps an angel might be a more appropriate name for you." His smile was warm and flirtatious as he said it and it made her blush.

"I'm not that either. Tea?" she quickly diverted the conversation.

"I'll take a raincheck. Perhaps it's better if you get some sleep. We have a lot of work ahead of us in the morning. I'll send the driver to pick you up." Pascale turned and walked towards the exit, briefly looking back as he opened the door. "We're all sinners, Jorja. Works in progress. Don't assume your mistakes automatically lead to death."

CHAPTER TEN

Jorja's eyes snapped open. Blinking twice, she lay still in the darkness of her bedroom, listening. The lock in the door to her apartment softly snapped in place. She wasn't imagining it. Someone was in her apartment. Listening for footsteps she remained still, her back turned toward her bedroom entrance. She slowly rolled back to look over her shoulder, hoping to see better, but the sheets rustled noisily and she stopped. Again she listened. Terror ripped through her body, her senses suddenly flooded with danger. But everything had gone quiet. Her mind searched for answers, concluding that perhaps she had woken up when the intruder was leaving. Perhaps he had already been inside while she was asleep. The thought made her skin crawl and she briefly shut her eyes to shake it off. Listening with more intent, her heartbeat pulsed noisily in her ears, rushing her blood to her head to where she needed to blink several times to see through the darkness. When she detected no sound or motion of any kind, she moved to get up.

As she got to her feet and cautiously tippy-toed toward the doorway, another sound came from just outside her bedroom as the intruder bumped into the glass coffee table. She knew because she had done it herself when she got up to fetch water in the middle of the night.

She fell back against the wall, pinning her head back against the hard surface, her heart suddenly in her throat. He was still there.

She readied her body to ward off an attack. But it was too late. A gloved hand closed over her mouth while his body pushed her back against the wall. Dressed in a dark gray hoodie, the outlines of his face barely visible in the dark shadows of her room, she tried fighting back. But he was too strong. Using his full body, he pinned her to the wall, pushed his cheek up against hers as he whispered close to her ear.

"Shh, it's me, don't make a sound."

In the pale moonlit room, his face suddenly lined up with hers as he fixed his gaze on her frightened eyes, his hand still over her mouth. When she recognized him, his mouth moved to her ear once more.

"They're listening. We have to get out of here."

Questions flooded her mind but she didn't argue. She trusted Pascale.

Once again his face was mere inches away from hers, his eyes silently checking if he could let go. She nodded, and he slowly released his hand from her mouth, his body still pinned to hers, the strength of it sending butterflies through her stomach. As if he sensed the effect it had on her, his eyes twinkling, he slowly eased up and let her go. Eager to escape his power, she dashed to snatch up her clothes from the nearby chair, bundling it up against her body as she stooped to collect her shoes on the way out. Like two cat burglars in the night, they hastily moved through the dark space, carefully opening the door to escape down the hallway. Passing the guest elevator, Pascale led her down the hall and around the corner to where the service elevator's doors had been wedged open. As soon as the doors closed behind them, Jorja spoke for the first time.

"Pascale, what's going on? Who's listening?"

But his eyes were on the overhead lights as the elevator ascended a further ten floors.

"Hurry, get dressed."

She did as he said and hastily stepped into her jeans before she pulled her navy sweater over her head and slipped her feet into her sneakers.

"Pascale, tell me, what's going on and why are we going up instead of down?" she begged as she pulled the heel of her shoe in place.

But still Pascale didn't answer—his focus remained on their escape and moments later, the elevator doors parted to usher them out on top of the roof. Warm air hit them the instant they ran out onto the rooftop, the markings of a helipad painted beneath their feet.

"Now what?" Jorja said, noticing there was no other way off the roof.

"This way."

She didn't hesitate and followed Pascale to one of the rooftop corners where two rappelling ropes were already fixed to a steel anchor in the concrete floor.

"You've been busy," she said as she stepped into the harness and coiled the rope around her hand to start her descent. "Any reason why we can't use the rear exit instead though?"

"I told you, they're everywhere. Now, hurry up! We have less than a minute before they close in on us."

Pascale went over the edge of the fifteen-story apartment block first, his body gliding down the side of the building with swift ease. Close behind him, Jorja fed the rope through the belay device, her bare hands burning against the cord. A quick glance between her feet showed that Pascale had already reached the ground. She was only approaching the halfway point. From somewhere in the distance above her head she heard voices atop the roof and she briefly looked up to find three shadowy bodies peering down at her.

"Jorja, hurry!" Pascale shouted from below, holding her rope steady to facilitate her descent.

But, try as she might, without gloves to protect her hands from the rope's friction, she struggled to speed up her downward climb. She was running out of time.

"Jorja, hurry up! I've got you, just drop down!" Pascale yelled.

Moments later the rope swayed vigorously, nearly knocking her head into the wall. She clung to the cord, tried to steady herself by pushing her feet into the wall. But it was pointless. The men were intentionally trying to shake her off the rope.

Then they suddenly stopped.

"Now! You're almost there!" Pascale shouted again, keeping a watchful eye on the men on the roof.

Jorja's heart pounded in her throat. Pain shot from her hand that fed the rope, tears sat shallow in her eyes. Below her Pascale stood ready, his arms up as if he could catch her. Resisting the pain in her hand, she dropped down, free falling as fast as the rope would allow. Then it started; the grinding vibrations that rippled down through the cord. They were trying to cut her rope loose. Panic threatened to set in as she looked down to where Pascale stood waiting for her. Lit up by the pale moonlight, he stared up at her, his eyes filled with dread.

"I've got you, Jorja, just keep going," he yelled toward her.

As she tried to speed up her descent, the rope seared into the soft flesh of her palm, sending her body into an instant reflex to stop.

"You're almost down, Jorja, don't stop now, keep going!" he encouraged.

But, it was too late. Above her, the rope's tension released and tumbled down towards her.

Her body became light as air as she plunged toward the ground.

Facing certain injury—possibly even death—adrenaline surged through her veins. She called out to her Savior as she tumbled three stories through the air. Survival kicked in—or, more likely, divine intervention—and she grabbed onto Pascale's rope that still dangled next to her. Her body jerked to a halt, pain ripping through her wounded hands as her bodyweight tugged on the tendons in her neck and shoulder. She slammed against the concrete wall, momentarily losing her breath. For a brief second the rope slipped through her tired fingers before she managed to tighten her grip and bring her body to a stop. She no longer felt pain. All she felt was relief. With her feet coiled around the rope, she steadied herself, providing a few seconds of respite to gain full control. A quick glance below her told her she was only one story above the ground.

"Come on, come on!" Pascale yelled, his voice filled with new hope as she dangled just out of reach above him.

But, as was the case with her rope, the men sliced through her lifeline and she plummeted to the ground.

CHAPTER ELEVEN

Jorja's body thumped on top of Pascale, who had intentionally positioned himself to break her fall. He fell backward, groaning under the impact as his body slammed into the ground before momentum deposited her next to him.

Lightheadedly, she scrambled to her feet, looking back to find Pascale still flat on his back. "Pascale, get up. We have to go!"

He didn't move.

She checked if he was breathing, relieved to find that he was. Again she called for him to get up and still he didn't respond.

Panic set in. He was alive, that much she knew. She dropped to her knees next to him, all the while looking in all directions to see if their attackers were near.

"Pascale, say something. Are you okay? Please get up!" she pleaded, tapping him lightly on the cheek. He groaned, then coughed as air filled his lungs—the fall had knocked his wind out.

Relief washed over her and she uttered a quick prayer of thanks as she jumped to her feet, pulling him by his arm to help him up. Her eyes darted to the dark corners around them, grateful to find that the men hadn't caught up to them yet.

"We have to go, Pascale! I'm sure these guys will be here any moment. Come on!" she yelled, pinning her gaze on the dark spaces around them.

When she looked over at Pascale he was attempting to push himself off the ground but flinched when he tried using his arm. He tried again and groaned in agony as pain shot through his limb, telling her that his arm had been badly injured—or possibly broken.

"Okay, I've got you. Lean on me," Jorja said as she rushed to his side and wedged her body under his to pull him to his feet. "Are you okay to walk? Does anything else hurt?"

"Only my ego," he briefly joked before he continued in a more serious tone. "I'm okay, but we need to get out of here." Clutching his arm to his chest, he pushed his chin out toward the adjacent building. "Over there, I have a car parked in the basement."

Wasting no time, hidden by the dark shadows of the night, they hurried across the side street and around the back of the building. When they arrived at the locked entrance, Pascale reached inside his back pocket in search of the electronic card that would release the large iron gate that closed off the underground garage. Instead, he found the card had been broken in two.

"No-no-no!" he exclaimed as he assessed the damage between his fingers. "It must have broken in the fall." Holding his injured arm to his chest, he tried pulling up on the locked gate, shaking it in frustration as it remained locked.

Next to him, Jorja was quick to catch on, her eyes already scanning the electronic lock on the nearby wall.

"It's fine, I've got it," she quickly announced and turned to scour the area for something sharp to jimmy the electronic box.

"Will this work?" Pascale asked where he produced a multitool from a fanny pack that was concealed by his hoodie.

She smiled. "I can't say I saw that one coming. You are full of surprises tonight, aren't you?" She flipped it open and started on the small screws that fixed the locking device to the wall.

"If nothing else, I like to be prepared," he said, then moved to sneak a look around the corner of the building.

By the time he was next to her again, she had removed the cap of the box to reveal several colored wires. In just a few seconds, she had sorted through them before she used the bladed tool on the gadget and sliced through two of the wires. With care, she switched the open ends of the unlike wires and held the coppery bits together. The gate whirred up into the roof.

"I guess it pays to be friends with a master thief," Pascale mocked playfully. Where the gated garage door had already lifted off the ground to allow a large enough gap for them to comfortably fit through, they ducked underneath. Inside, the basement was dark and quiet and Pascale led the way between the parking bays.

"The car is over there," Pascale said, as he ran toward it.

A slick white sedan stood waiting in the spot where Pascale had left it and he tossed the keys to Jorja.

"I reckon you'll do a better job of it than me." He was still clutching his injured arm.

But, no sooner had they gotten into the car and started the engine, when the first bullet loudly clanked against the car's wheel cap. Jorja flattened the gas pedal, spinning the car's rear wheels to release clouds of blue smoke all around them as they sped off in the car.

Soon, two men on foot appeared out of nowhere amongst the smoke. As they closed in on the car, both aimed their guns directly at Jorja and Pascale.

Pascale crouched down and took cover behind the dashboard then retrieved a gun from beneath the driver's seat. As Jorja spun the car around and raced toward the exit, another bullet slammed into the rear of the vehicle. The car's tires screeched noisily, narrowly dodging the flying bullets that now rained on them from behind.

With his shooting arm out of action, Pascale took aim with his healthy arm. But, as he fired toward their attackers, his aim was off and he missed. Once more he tried, but it yielded the same result. Frustrated with his drawback, and choosing to instead save his ammunition, he abandoned the task, grunting as he receded into his seat.

Desperate to shake their attackers, Jorja took a sharp corner, her eyes fixed on the rearview mirror as they chased after them. Escaping the attack claimed her full attention. She raced the vehicle through the entrance toward the road, turning the nose of the car up a side street the moment they got out of the building. In the brief moment she managed to get out of their line of fire, the bullets ceased. Relief poked its head out for a mere moment before they spotted the large black SUV that suddenly turned in behind them.

"Turn left!" Pascale yelled.

Jorja followed his directions. Her hands gripped firmly around the steering wheel, her body tense and pinned to the back of her seat. The car sped through the dark roads as she followed each of Pascale's commands until they could no longer see the SUV behind them.

"I think we've lost them," Jorja said, her eyes darting between the car's mirrors as they reached the highway that led out of Abu Dhabi.

"Good, because I think I might have just injured my arm in a few more places."

"Yeah, we're going to have to get that seen to."

"It will have to wait."

Jorja peered into the dark night. "Now what? I don't see anything but desert for miles around us. Are you sure you know where we're going?"

"Have I ever let you down?" he glanced sideways.

"No, you haven't."

"There's a small airfield about five miles up the road," he added.

Jorja flattened her foot on the gas. "Perhaps this is the perfect time to tell me who nearly killed us back there," she said.

"I'm loath to admit it but they're meant to be on our side." He winced in pain as he moved his injured arm into a more comfortable position.

"You mean to tell me they were Interpol agents?"

"I'm afraid so."

"This has to be a mistake. Surely it's just a misunderstanding."

"I wish it was but sadly, it's the brutal truth."

"That's just great." Sarcasm laced her voice as she continued. "Your own people are now trying to kill us."

Pascale nodded. "I guess the cat's out of the proverbial bag."

"What about Harry, and Mo, and even Kalihm? We should let them know. Perhaps they can—"

"They're all in on it," he cut her off.

A frown pulled between Jorja's eyes as Pascale's words rendered her speechless. "It can't be. I mean, how can you be certain? None of this makes any sense. Why would your own team want to kill us?"

Pascale rested his head back, shutting his eyes in an effort to control the pain in his arm as he spoke.

"I went by the office after I left you earlier—to take a look at what was on the flash drive that Diego gave us. There was a crossword app open on Harry's computer and it struck me as odd. I mean, does he look like a kid who likes doing crosswords? Turns out my hunch was right—it was a communication tool."

Jorja frowned. "I don't follow."

"Sometimes hackers and criminals use gaming apps to secretly communicate messages to one another and often, these apps automatically erase the messages after twenty-four hours. It's a very simple but effective way to safeguard their scheming."

"Harry used crossword puzzles to communicate with someone," Jorja slowly caught on.

"It wasn't hard to find the messages—even with them being obscured in crossword clues. He's been feeding intel on me. This entire operation, every step I've taken, every plan I've set in motion. He's been passing it on via a private server. Worse is, they're all in on it. My entire team has been squealing on me. I found several messages sent between all three of them."

"To whom? Who are they reporting this to?"

"I have no idea. All I know is that he goes by the name Geppetto. Unfortunately my poking around triggered a firewall and well, here we are."

After a small pause, Jorja finally spoke. "Tell me it was worth it though. What's on the flash drive?"

CHAPTER TWELVE

Harry's fingers danced over his keyboard. Underneath his desk, his knee nervously bounced up and down.

"Nothing, absolutely nothing," he said to Mo who had been pacing the space in front of Harry's desk. "It's as if they vanished from the face of the planet. There isn't a single traffic or security cam anywhere in the city that picked them up."

"It's impossible," Mo said. "Keep checking. Pascale is most likely injured—I saw her falling on him. They couldn't have gotten far."

"Well, I'm telling you, I can't find them."

Mo slammed his flat hand on Harry's desk. "You might as well sign our death certificates, mate. You were supposed to track them."

"And you weren't supposed to let them get away in the first place, Mo! So, it's as much your fault as it is mine."

The space between the two men went quiet as they each contemplated the dooming position they now found themselves in.

"You're right, sorry," Mo said, as he rubbed his large hand over his bald head and stepped away from the desk. "If we don't do something soon to find them you and I will end up dead in a ditch or worse, back behind bars. I can't go back, Harry, I can't. This was our ticket out of here, man, our one opportunity to break free from the Program. I want to be free, choose who I want to work with. Being forced to work for the feds is no different from being in jail. We're still under their control."

Harry sighed and pushed his chair back on its wheels, jumped to his feet, and clasped his hands in the nape of his neck. "I know, but this has turned out to be a giant mess, Mo. I never thought I'd become a mole, a Judas. Pascale doesn't deserve this, neither does Jorja. She's actually really cool. We were just meant to keep an eye on them, lead them down the wrong paths. Killing them was never part of the deal. A deal I didn't want to make in the first place!"

"I know, but we did what we needed to do. It's not like we had a choice. Our backs were up against the wall, Harry. Anyone in our position would have done the same and I refuse to feel guilty about it. Who are we to now question Geppetto anyway? From where I stand he's the one holding the real keys to our freedom, not some government agency or Pascale, as nice as the guy might be. We knew it was risky when Geppetto approached us back then but we signed up for it regardless. Because it was the only way we would get our freedom back. Now, we have to finish the job."

Mo inhaled deeply then exhaled slowly, repeating it a few times as if he tried to rid his big muscular body from his plaguing conscience. When he came back from his cleansing ritual, he asked, "Why was Pascale on your computer anyway? You said he got caught in the booby trap. How did that happen?"

Harry, who was now standing with his thumbs hooked into the belt loops of his ripped black jeans, shook his head as he rolled his eyes. "Firstly, it's not called a booby trap. We're not out in a war zone somewhere, Mo. This is highly sophisticated cyber—"

"Yeah, whatever, kid. Save me the shop talk and cut to the chase."

Harry plonked himself back behind his desk. "Fine, you wouldn't get it anyway. From what I can tell, Pascale accessed a flash drive. Unfortunately, he cleaned up after himself and deleted all the cookies and the cache. It will take hours of digging to find out what was on it. Heck, I'm not even sure I can."

Mo paced the room again. "Keep digging, Harry. Every security camera, dash cam, whatever it takes. And search through those files of yours and find out what he had on that flash drive, before Geppetto finds out Pascale and Jorja got away." He overturned the nearby chair as he snarled. "Why did Pascale have to be so insanely smart by digging around on your computer? Everything was running smoothly."

"Yeah well, he's smart but at least he hasn't cracked the files yet."

"You're right. Check in with Kalihm and tell him what went down tonight. Tell him to watch his back. As long as those files are safe, we can get back on track and stay one step ahead of Pascale, just like we've been doing all along."

Kalihm parked the gunmetal gray rental car in the alley along the back of the nightclub like he had always done when he visited the club to meet with Franz. He glanced at the clock on the dashboard. He was early. The club wouldn't be closed for at least another forty minutes. In the dark silence of his car, with his head tilted back against his seat's headrest and his eyes lightly closed, he waited for Franz.

A glass bottle fell and broke somewhere behind him and he jerked upright, firming his grip around the gun in his lap as he did so. In his rearview mirror, a drunk couple laughed noisily at the top of the alley, the pale moonlight dancing off the shards of glass by their feet.

"Stupid kids," Kalihm muttered under his breath, shuffling restlessly as he kept an eye on them.

Soon the young couple moved along and crossed the street to where they disappeared out of sight.

Quick surveillance and another scan at the clock revealed that he still had twenty minutes left before Franz was due to join him in the car. Plenty of time for another little catnap, he thought as he subconsciously glanced at the manilla envelope that contained Franz's files on the seat next to him. But, barely five minutes later, another noise had his eyes flash open. This time, the noise was right behind the car.

His eyes darted frantically between the rearview mirrors, but everything was quiet around him and he restlessly shuffled upright in his seat. The solid grip of his gun pushed hard against the soft flesh of his palm as he readied himself against a possible threat, and when the rearview mirrors still didn't reveal anything, he turned around to look behind the car, then back across the hood of the car. Still, he didn't see anything.

For a moment, he wondered if it might have been his imagination, concluding that it was most probably a rat rummaging for food at the nearby dumpster. He paused and listened. Still nothing, and he instantly relaxed his shoulders. But, as he once again prepared to settle into his nap, another noise told him he wasn't imagining it—nor did it sound like a rat in a dumpster. When yet again it sounded like someone had tossed a small stone against the side of his car, he gave a sudden jerk of his head to look where the noise came from. But when he still didn't see anything, he got out of the car instead.

With his fingers tightly gripped around his gun, he stepped out of the car, briefly paused next to his door, then slowly moved around the rear of the car. His eyes darted between the dark shadows of the alley and behind the dumpster as he slowly approached the passenger side of his vehicle.

Still he didn't see anything. He stopped, listened for movement, then heard a sudden shuffling behind him before something hard clobbered him against the back of his head.

He fell forward and onto his knees, unable to hold onto the gun as it slipped out of his hands and slid underneath the dumpster. Slightly off balance, he tried standing up, but another hard knock rendered him disoriented and he fell face-first to the ground. Next to him, he was aware of the passenger door opening then, he heard the rustling of the envelope before the door quickly shut again. Footsteps shuffled noisily next to him and he tried turning around to get a look at his attacker but couldn't. Moments later a piece of duct tape glued his mouth shut quickly followed by a black hood that covered his head before he was dragged to his feet and tossed in the trunk of his car. Just as swiftly his hands were bound behind his back before the tailgate locked him inside.

CHAPTER THIRTEEN

The private airfield was located about an hour out of Abu Dhabi and accessible only via a narrow, off-the-beaten-track road that ran between a valley of large dunes. Apart from a single hangar and a runway that was just long enough to accommodate a small two-or four-seater plane, there was nothing much of anything else for miles in any direction. It was as if it was a little hidden aircraft oasis in the middle of a desert.

When the pair stepped out of the car, Pascale went to the side of the hangar where a retina scanner opened the door.

"It's not much, but there's coffee and food over there and a bathroom back in that corner," he said as they walked in.

"You live here?"

He laughed. "Not unless I'm forced to. It's a safe house of sorts, available to undercover agents when they need to lie low for a bit. They've got them in locations all over the world. We should be safe here for a couple of days until we figure out how we're going to get Diego his paintings."

Jorja stared at the small two-seater plane. "I'm assuming this is at your disposal too. I didn't know you could fly."

Pascale scrunched up his face and cocked his head to one side. "It's available, but I can't really fly. I mean, I've done half the flight hours required to pass but unfortunately my assignment took me away from completing the rest. I always thought I'd catch up some time in the future."

"But, if this is a secret hideout, surely they'll know to come look for us here."

"That is highly unlikely. Aside from me knowing about it, it hasn't been in use for nearly a decade. It's never a good idea to put all your cards on the table and this one is a little secret I've intentionally kept in my back pocket for situations precisely like this." He walked over to her, clutching his arm. "We're safe here, trust me. Besides, we won't be here for long. Now, do you think you can help me pop my arm back in its socket, please?"

His request had Jorja in a tailspin. "You want *me* to do that? No, I can't. We need to get you to a doctor."

Pascale's eyes locked onto hers. "I don't trust anyone out there, Jorja. You're my only option."

Jorja sighed and ran her hands through her hair. "Fine, but don't hold me responsible if I break your arm."

He laughed. "I won't, promise."

She paused to center herself. "Tell me what to do."

"Grab my wrist and pull my arm toward you and straight, firmly, and quickly."

She nodded before she rolled her shoulders back to loosen the tension in her neck. "Okay, I'm ready."

Positioning her stance, she took hold of his wrist and did as he had instructed. Pascale moaned in pain when it didn't succeed, biting the back of his fist to cope with the pain.

"I'm sorry! I told you I couldn't do it. Honestly, I think we can find a backstreet doctor or a nurse somewhere and pay them to keep quiet," she said as she tried to persuade him.

"No, we can't risk being seen. You can do it. Try again. This time, align it as you pull back." He steadied himself. "I'm ready. Go for it."

Jorja positioned herself once more, took a deep breath, and pulled back on his arm. Pascale's dislocated shoulder popped back into place, leaving him out of breath as he fell back against the nearby wall to keep himself stable.

"Did it work?"

He nodded as he steadied his breathing to gain control over the pain, then pushed himself away from the wall.

"You did great, thank you." He leaned in and gently kissed her on the cheek. "You're a life saver, Jorja Rose, thank you." He spoke gently then, turned to get an ice pack from the small fridge behind him.

"Are you okay? Can I do anything?" she said when he slumped down onto the single blue sofa that stood nearby.

"I'll be fine, don't worry. Nothing a bit of ice and a couple of painkillers won't fix. We have about two hours until daybreak. It should be enough time to rest my shoulder and get the swelling down."

Jorja flopped onto the sofa next to him, resting her head back against it. "I could sleep for a thousand years," she said as she closed her eyes.

Sounding as tired as she did, Pascale replied. "I know the feeling, but we can't. Have you forgotten that we have a madman who's forcing us to do his dirty work for him? We have three paintings to steal, remember? Not to mention dodging the bullets of those traitors."

"I'm aware, so out with it. What do we have to do so we can finally get out of this mess and back to some semblance of a normal life again?"

"Normal? I don't even know what that means." Pascale chuckled. "I mean, do you honestly think our lives are ever going to be normal again, Jorja? Even if we do get Diego's paintings back, and trust me, it's a huge if, he's not going to just let us go. He's a criminal, Gerard's a criminal, and whoever he reports to is an even bigger criminal. All of them protected by a bunch of crooked politicians and apparently now also a corrupt criminal justice system. They have too much at stake and too much to lose. So no matter which way we slice it, it will take a miracle to steal any of these paintings—even for you. We have no backup, no resources, nothing."

Jorja smoothed her hair back behind her ears. "Then I guess we need to trust God's hand in this, don't we? I've done it before, and I can do it again. Besides, you are clearly underestimating me. I too haven't played all the cards in my hand."

Pascale's eyes had gone from being filled with despair to finding new hope and courage in Jorja's words. The corners of his mouth curled up.

"I'm too scared to ask," he said, "so, how about I show you what we're up against and then you can tell me how the pros do it? I'd love for you to prove me wrong," he said with teasing eyes.

From within a small safe that was concealed behind a wall-mounted tool cabinet, Pascale retrieved a laptop and inserted the memory stick into the port. Three unnamed yellow computer folders flashed onto the screen. He paused and looked back at Jorja where she stood observing over his shoulder.

"Ready?"

"As I'll ever be."

He highlighted all three files and opened them collectively, waiting for Jorja's reaction as, one by one, images of the three paintings popped onto the computer screen. As he predicted, Jorja gasped then leaned in to have a closer look, blinking as if her eyes were deceiving her.

"I warned you didn't I?"

She stepped back, her hands on her hips as she paced the small space behind him.

"I don't even know how this is possible," she said. "Why now? Why like this? All those years, searching for that golden egg. That one opportunity that proves your worth and gains you ultimate credibility and a massive payday. In my entire career as an art thief that moment never came.

And now, suddenly, here it is. Three golden eggs all at once."

Jorja was visibly shaken as she leaned in to have another look. "No, it's not possible. It can't be. They're not even supposed to exist anymore." She buried her face in her hands as she stepped away and anxiously started pacing again. "Not to mention that stealing is a sin! I'm literally going to break one of the cardinal laws of my religious foundation. And for what? Twenty years it's taken me to clean up my life, walk away from all things evil and wham, I get forced back into being someone I hate." A lonely tear ran down her cheek as she stood with her back toward Pascale.

"I know, Jorja. I've been wrestling with this very thing for years. But no matter how many times I've begged God to lead me into a different career, it's where He wants me, where He needs me. On the right side of the law. And sometimes it takes us doing the unthinkable to stop corruption and bring these criminals to justice. Perhaps God is using this moment to test your heart by taking you back to that place of sin before He can properly deliver you from it. Far be it from me to offer any theological insight, but I'd like to believe that this time around, because your heart is in the right place, God offers you grace. The intention behind the theft has changed and that should count for something."

Jorja swept the tear away before she turned to face Pascale. "You really think that? You think God will forgive me for stealing these paintings?"

"I believe that He understands the situation we're finding ourselves in, yes, but, make sure you guard your heart to not let the thrill of the heist consume you. Keep your eyes on Jesus. It's the only way I've managed to do it all these years."

Jorja closed the space between them and lightly touched Pascale's shoulder. "Thank you." She smiled then let her eyes trail to the images on the computer screen.

"Judging from the fact that all three of these paintings are Biblical depictions, I think you might be right. It's as if God's gently reminding us to keep our focus on Him."

CHAPTER FOURTEEN

S he studied the paintings on the screen. "Do you think they're originals?"

"I think, at this point, it doesn't really matter. But if they are it makes perfect sense why Diego is so desperate to get his hands on them. Individually, they're worth millions. As a collection..." he blew out a puff of air between his lips.

"They're worth a massive fortune," Jorja finished his sentence, her eyes still fixed on the images.

"Exactly, and a major criminal like Diego Cortez would definitely need big ticket collateral items like these to keep his business going."

Jorja took a few steps back, her hands clasped behind her neck as she threw her head back. "Okay, what do we know about each painting? Let's start with the Rembrandt, *The*

Storm on the Sea of Galilee. We know it's one of the most valuable missing works of art in the world. Painted by Rembrandt in 1633, a biblical scene where Jesus is at sea on a boat with His disciples and calms a storm."

"Correct. It was last seen in 1990 in the Isabella Stewart Gardner Museum in Boston, Massachusetts. Stolen by two robbers disguised in police uniforms in what remains, to this day, one of the biggest art-heists in history. No disrespect to parties present, of course." He smiled.

"Of course. None taken," she smiled back before he continued.

"This painting was stolen along with twelve others, never to be seen again. Two guys disguised themselves as cops, walked in and simply walked out an hour later."

"Talk about genius," Jorja said, then added, "It's going to be a real challenge to track these down, Pascale. I won't even know where to start looking." She sighed.

Pascale chortled as he opened up another folder and dragged it to the middle of the screen. "Lucky for us, we don't have to look too far. Turns out Diego has already done the hard work for us. How, I don't know, but he has locations on all three of our targets."

He clicked his trackpad to open one of the documents.

Once again Jorja gasped as she read the words on the screen. "You're not serious! Venice. You mean to tell me that this painting has somehow ended up in a cathedral in Venice?"

"Not just any cathedral, *the* Scuola Grande di San Rocco, founded in 1478 with more than sixty Tintoretto paintings still perfectly preserved in their original state."

"I've only ever heard of these paintings. A perfect pictorial cycle illustrating episodes from the New and Old Testament. It makes perfect sense for *The Storm on the Sea of Galilee* to be amongst them. I wish I knew how it made its way from a Boston museum to a Venice cathedral at the hands of thieves. Actually, strike that. I don't want to know," Jorja said.

"Yeah, well, it could be anywhere inside the cathedral. That's the part we still have to figure out."

"We'll figure it out. Which one is next?" Jorja asked.

"I'll stick with another easy one and leave the best for last," Pascale said with a mischievous smile. "Just in case you feel the need to kill the messenger." He switched his computer pointer back to one of the other images, Jorja leaning in over his shoulder, and enlarged the image on the screen.

"Caravaggio's *Nativity with St. Francis and St. Lawrence*," Jorja said as she studied the image. "A nativity of Jesus painted in 1609. A brilliant piece of art. I never thought I would ever have the privilege of laying eyes on it, never mind stealing it."

"And hopefully we're successful. This one could be a little bit of a challenge. It's been missing since 1969 when it was stolen from the Oratory of Saint Lawrence in Palermo. They suspected that the Sicilian Mafia was involved but they've never even come close to finding it."

"Yet our dear friend, Diego, knows where it is."

"Why wouldn't he? They're all in the same line of business, aren't they? Art is one of the main currencies among the criminals of this nature. It moves between them like money trades hands in a street café. It's how they either cover up their crimes, or get themselves out of being killed."

"Or make millions if you're the middleman like Züber was," Jorja added.

"Exactly. I'm just surprised that the *Gardiens* haven't found a way to own it yet. Want to know where it is?"

"Is the Pope Catholic?" Jorja mocked rhetorically.

"Well, funny you should ask. As it turns out, that's precisely where it is." Pascale paused.

"No! You don't...tell me you're joking. I am not breaking into the Vatican," Jorja exclaimed. "I thought you said this was an easy one."

"I'm afraid you don't have a choice. That's precisely where it is. Somewhere in the Vatican, probably right under the Pope's nose," he let out a half-suppressed laugh.

Jorja's hands were in her hair as she paced back and forth before she eventually said, "Okay, there's nothing to panic about. We've got this. So it's the Vatican. How hard can it be? Right?" She looked at Pascale who sat watching her with amusement. "Why are you so calm about this?" she asked.

A smile broke on his face. "Because, I told you I'm leaving the best for last. Those were the easy ones." He turned to face his laptop again as he clicked on the final photo. "Last, but by no means least, the *Ecce Homo* by Anthony van Dyck. Painted circa 1620, a beautiful oil on canvas depicting a scourged Christ in a crown of thorns, whom Pilate shows to the Jewish people."

Jorja studied the painting. "I don't know this one," she said.

"Not many people do and that's because it went missing during WWII. It was part of a Warsaw sculptor's private collection but it was believed to have been almost completely destroyed—or looted—when the Germans invaded Poland. Although never confirmed, evidence suggested that it made it into Hitler's private loot which, of course, has never been found."

Jorja let out an exasperated grunt. "Okay, lay it on me. Where does Diego Cortez think this painting is because half the world has been scouring the earth in search of Hitler's missing fortunes, with zero success, I might add."

"Apparently, he knows exactly where it is; the painting at least, not Hitler's fortune." He smiled before he continued. "Diego believes this painting made it into a German banker's private vault." He paused then added, "And, by the sounds of it, he's spent a ton of money to protect it. Also, I hope you can ski, because we're heading into the Swiss Alps."

CHAPTER FIFTEEN

I n the dead of night, within the safe confines of their hideout, Jorja and Pascale pored over the information on the flash drive. Recalling Diego's threatening conversation, there was no time to waste, and the pair set about tackling their reconnaissance.

But, merely a few hours later, as the new day broke, danger wasn't far away and a distant noise suddenly caught Pascale's attention. With his body upright and in full alert, he stopped to listen more closely.

"What's wrong?" Jorja whispered, only to be met by Pascale's index finger over his mouth as his other hand moved to pick up his gun. A few swift paces toward the door had him pressing his ear up against the wall of the hangar.

Outside, amplified by the surrounding dunes, the wheels of

at least one vehicle rolled down the road toward them, the soft purring of its engine clearly audible in the stillness of the early morning.

"They found us," Pascale said quietly, pulling the flash drive from the computer and pressing a single button that started an automated sequence to delete their digital tracks.

While the sequence ran, he flipped a switch in the kitchen to reveal a concealed shelf behind one of the walls. Neatly arranged inside it was a collection of ammunition available for his choosing. He reached in and took out two more handguns, several magazines, and extra bullets before passing one of the guns to Jorja. Moving with haste he tucked the other gun in the waistband of his pants then retrieved a small backpack and buried the ammunition inside before he slung it over his shoulder.

"Let's go!" he beckoned to Jorja.

But, when they reached the door to exit the hangar in the hope of making a run for the car, he stopped dead in his tracks.

Along the boundaries of the property, the approaching vehicle had stopped and light footsteps crunched on the loose gravel that was intentionally placed in a ring around the hangar—an early detection signal to warn them of approaching danger.

It was too late to escape by car.

Somewhat flustered, Pascale searched for another way out as the footsteps drew closer. Out of options, surrounded by the enemy, Jorja and Pascale knew they were outnumbered —and trapped.

"You said you can fly, right?" Jorja hinted.

"No, I said I couldn't fly. It's been years since I sat in the cockpit of a plane," Pascale objected.

"Well, there's no other way out of this hangar or airfield but up. Even if we did make it to the car in one piece, we most likely won't get past them on the road. The runway is the only way out of here and that means we're going to have to fly this plane if we want to stay alive."

There was no time for Pascale to protest as the enemy had already reached the door to the building. Jorja was on the plane first, soon joined as Pascale stepped into the cockpit from the other side of the aircraft.

"This is a bad idea, Jorja. I have no idea how to fly this thing."

His hand moved to start the plane, pausing briefly as his mind spun out of control in a desperate effort to remember what he was meant to do next.

"I don't want to cause more panic but they're about to burst through that door, Pascale."

"You do realize it's suicide taking off without having done the necessary safety checks. We don't even know if this plane has any fuel."

"I am prepared to take my chances, so get going," Jorja responded, desperate to hide her angst.

"I can't believe I'm saying this, but I'm inclined to agree. Here goes nothing," Pascale said as he started the motor and gently pulled back on the throttle to increase the engine's power.

The propeller whirred noisily in front of them and Jorja kept her watchful gaze on the entrance door that was positioned to her right.

Gunshots dented the metal as bullets rained down onto the door in an attempt to break through the lock of the reinforced steel door.

"We need to get out of here, Pascale!" Jorja yelled.

He instantly reacted by pressing down a red button on a small remote control that dangled from the throttle handle.

The large hangar door in front of the plane slowly rolled up—too slowly to either of their liking, but they held firm.

Four armed men pushed their way through the hangar's entrance, instantly rushing toward the stationary two-seater aircraft.

"Come on, come on!" Jorja yelled at the hangar door as if to hurry it along so they could get going.

She looked cautiously over her shoulder and fixed her eyes to Mo's face where he had led the small group of soldiers into the hangar.

As he took aim at her, their gaze met and she saw in Mo's eyes a cold determination she didn't expect him to have. Sadness filled her heart and she shot up a prayer that God would stir his heart to stop.

But Mo didn't back down. He took stance behind the couch and aimed his gun directly at the plane's fuel tank.

Death knocked hard and fast and, in an attempt to buy more time and ward off the imminent onslaught, Jorja was quick to find a way out. Grabbing the flare gun from a cubby next to her, she opened her window and fired an emergency flare into the couch. Instantly the couch burst into flames. Smoke filled the space in front of Mo and his men and drew a temporary smoke curtain between them and the airplane. As Mo and his men coughed in the surrounding clouds of smoke that now bellowed from the burning couch, the small team of soldiers was forced to drop their aim. The slight window of opportunity provided just enough time for the hangar door to open a gap large enough for the plane to fit underneath, and Pascale released the brakes. The lightweight plane launched out of the hangar, speeding onto the runway as they raced against time to get it up in the air.

But Mo and his men were right behind them and the first bullet whistled past the plane's wing. Pascale pulled back on the throttle to increase speed, nearly stalling the plane in doing so. True to Mo's relentless warrior determination, several more bullets rained down on the light aircraft. With nearly enough speed to finally lift the plane's nose up into the air, a bullet slammed into the front wheel of the plane, instantly rupturing the tire. Chunks of rubber scattered onto the runway and a few shards got in the way of the landing wheels. The plane wobbled as its nose thumped down onto the tarmac, the now exposed metal from the damaged wheel grinding beneath the fuselage. Pascale groaned under the strain on his injured arm as he fought to stabilize the plane, his eyes pinned to the end of the runway that was fast drawing near. Desperate to lift the plane into the air he gave it his all, prayed for God to intervene, until he finally felt the wind lifting the nose off the ground to tilt them up toward the sky.

From the corner of her eye, Jorja marked the black SUV speeding toward them. The upper half of a man's body draped over the car's open window as he readied himself to fire his machine gun at them.

Jorja ducked, her body tense as adrenaline pumped into her veins. Once more she fought back and pushed the tip of her gun through the small window next to her. With no time to spare, she took aim at one of the vehicle's wheels and fired off a single shot. But the bullet missed its target.

Retaliation ensued and the foe sent several bullets back towards the plane. Bullets clanked noisily against parts of the aircraft just as it entirely lifted off the ground and launched into the air.

As the ground grew distant beneath them and the enemy faded into the background, Jorja and Pascale finally breathed again.

But more dire than Pascale's lack of skill in flying the plane, was that he had even less knowledge of the flight path that would take them to safety.

"I have no idea where I'm going," he commented once the plane's nose leveled just below the clouds.

Jorja searched the cabin around them. "And there isn't a map anywhere." She unclipped her seatbelt and wedged herself up on her knees to search the small space behind their seats.

"Nothing," she reported barely a minute later before she settled back into her seat and said, "judging from the sun's position, I know we're flying in a westerly direction. What lies west from Abu Dhabi?"

Pascale took a moment before he answered. "Qatar, we're heading toward Qatar."

"That's good, isn't it?"

"At least for now it is, but if I know Harry, and I do, he has already calculated possible escape routes on that computer of his. We're going to need to get to Qatar before they do."

"And, is that possible?"

"I think so. If I increase our speed, we can get there in under an hour. It will take them five by road so, by my estimation, we are at least four hours ahead of them. Once there, we can sneak onto the next flight from Doha to Rome."

CHAPTER SIXTEEN

With a steady altitude, feeling like they were in control and one step ahead, newfound hope filled the pair. But as Pascale increased the aircraft's speed, the engine discharged an unexpected sputter.

Pascale's arms tensed and stretched out in front of him, his hands fiercely clutching the yoke as his eyes darted between the gauges.

"What's wrong?" Jorja asked when she noticed him staring at the cockpit panel.

"That's what I'm trying to figure out. I have no idea what all these flashing lights mean."

Moments later an alarm went off.

"Pascale, what's happening?"

Pascale grew quiet, his attention now fully focused on keeping the plane in the air. But his efforts were futile when the engine suddenly cut out and the propeller came to a quick halt.

As the pair stared out toward the plane's nose, panic ripped through their minds and bodies.

Pascale's finger tapped aggressively against the glass on the fuel gauge. But the needle remained stuck on empty.

"We're out of fuel," he said, his voice low and onerous.

"They must have hit the fuel tank. Can you find somewhere to land?" Jorja's nose pressed against the window to better see the terrain below.

"I need power to land and right now we're gliding and losing altitude fast."

As the plane's nose dipped toward the moving earth beneath them, the pair was out of solutions, each quiet as they contemplated their fate.

To their left, the coastline drew further away from them as the plane headed over the Persian Gulf towards Qatar. Jorja stared nervously out the windows, her body now rigid in her seat as she waited for Pascale to say or do something. Overhead, another alarm suddenly went off, then another.

"Speak to me, Pascale, what's happening?"

Pascale groaned under the strain of the yoke as his efforts to veer the plane back to land turned up futile.

"It's not working," he groaned.

"What's not working?"

"The yoke, I can't seem to turn the plane."

In front of them, the plane's nose dove towards the fast-approaching ocean in front of them and Jorja instinctively took hold of the co-pilot yoke. She pulled back hard, desperate to help in any way she could.

But the aircraft was unresponsive.

In that moment, as the plane rapidly headed toward a watery crash, Jorja prayed that they would both survive.

Seconds later, the nose of the plane hit the water.

Inside the cabin, the momentum tossed Pascale and Jorja around as if they were inside a washing machine before the tail of the plane flipped over and turned the fuselage upside down. It slammed down hard onto the surface of the ocean, knocking both their winds out as water slowly poured into the plane.

Jorja got her bearings first and she called out to Pascale. But he didn't respond.

Her hand moved to shake his shoulder, still he wasn't responding.

"Pascale, wake up!"

Still Pascale was unresponsive.

Jorja tried again as she unclipped her seatbelt. When it released, her body thumped onto the roof of the plane. The sudden impact and shift of her weight caused the plane to sink further below the surface, forcing more water into the air pocketed cabin. Her hand moved to unclip Pascale's seatbelt, but it didn't budge.

"Pascale wake up! We have to get out of here!"

In a desperate effort to wake him up she slapped him across the face. His eyes fluttered ever so slightly.

"Pascale, wake up. Open your eyes!"

Around her, the water level rose to her waist while her fingers tugged desperately at the buckle on Pascale's seatbelt. But it remained stuck.

"What happened?" Pascale asked as he slowly came to.

"We crashed in the ocean and we're going to drown if we don't get out of here!"

When the seatbelt remained unyielding, she searched for something sharp between the floating debris inside the cabin.

But there was nothing.

She reached for her gun in her waistband, but quickly abandoned the notion as she realized the bullet might very well hit Pascale too.

"My fanny pack," Pascale groaned in an effort to remind her of the multitool he had inside.

Wasting no time she found the small device and sliced the bladed tool through the fibers of the safety straps. Pascale's body fell towards her, shifting the plane even deeper into the ocean. As the water level now pushed up under their chins, Jorja took out her gun and aimed it at the aircraft's window.

"Take a deep breath, Pascale," she instructed mere moments before the air pocket filled with water.

She fired two bullets into the window, then thrust her feet against the pane to break through the pierced sheet of glass. The window gave way easily, forcing a steady flow of water inside the plane. As the water's pressure pushed the plane further down below the surface and onto the ocean floor, Jorja and Pascale fought their way to the top.

Out of breath, their lungs aching to fill with air, they swam towards the light above them.

Jorja broke through the ocean surface, her body instantly reacting to the fresh air that filled her lungs. When she recovered, she turned to find Pascale.

But he was nowhere to be seen.

She turned her head in all directions to look for him, but couldn't see him anywhere. Realizing he hadn't made it to the surface she took a deep breath and dove under the water, twirling herself around as she desperately searched for him.

Several meters below, her eyes caught sight of his lifeless body drifting towards the ocean bed. She shot up to draw one quick breath before she dove down toward him.

Never once losing sight of him, the salty water burning at her eyes, she pushed through the water. Her hand closed around two of his fingers and she kicked harder until she fully took hold of his wrist. With hardly any oxygen left in her lungs, she pulled his body closer to her, then turned her eyes back towards the sun's rays that hit the ocean far above her head. Pascale's body dragged against the water and it took far more effort to get to the top than she had oxygen—or energy—left in her body. Several times she fought against her body's natural reflex to draw a breath and it felt as if her lungs were going to explode.

But as she neared the very last reserves of oxygen in her lungs, they burst through the water's surface.

Once again, Jorja's lungs filled with life, momentarily leaving her dizzy as oxygen surged through her body.

Next to her, still gripped in a lifeguard position under her forearm, the lower half of Pascale's body dragged through the water, his eyes shut, his face blue, his lungs unresponsive.

Pulling Pascale's body along next to her, she swam towards a piece of the plane's wings that had broken off during the crash. Straining to keep afloat, she fought to get his top half onto the debris. Finally succeeding, out of breath and her body weak beneath her, she kicked and pulled until her face was next to his.

He wasn't breathing.

Her lips closed over his mouth as she began CPR, slamming her fist on top of his chest after the first few breaths.

But still Pascale wasn't breathing.

"Don't you die on me, Pascale! You got me into this mess and I won't let you leave me to fight them off alone. You hear me? Breathe!"

She forced a few more breaths into his lungs, drove her palm down onto his chest as the other hand held onto the wreckage.

Pascale's body didn't respond.

Tears threatened to consume her but she kept at it, pushing air into his mouth while pushing against his chest as much as the awkward position would allow. Several minutes had already passed and still Pascale didn't breathe.

Ready to give up, she briefly stopped and screamed out into the Heavens.

"What more do you want from me, Lord? I said I was sorry. I don't know what else to do to make you forgive me. Please, Lord. I just want to have a normal life."

Tears flooded her eyes and ran down her face. Its sweet salty essence mixed with the salty sting of the ocean that surrounded them.

Several more times she banged her small fist against Pascale's chest. She kept at it, desperate not to give up as she breathed the air from her lungs into his. And as her body fell weak beneath the strain of keeping Pascale's body on top of the broken off wing of the plane, she dropped her head on top of his chest and sobbed in acceptance that he hadn't survived.

CHAPTER SEVENTEEN

Clinging to the floating debris, her head still on Pascale's chest, Jorja sobbed her heart out. She cried over losing Pascale and about the mess she had made of her life. Over the hollow traces of hopelessness that had now firmly taken root inside her soul and over the grim future she would once again be facing on her own. Tears filled with equal parts regret and shame dropped into the ocean bed around her as she cried out to the Heavens above. There was no saving her soul, not anymore. God would not forgive her any more than she could forgive herself. Sorrow and guilt overwhelmed her and the will to carry on threatened to give way to the clutches of death itself as her body grew more limp by the minute.

But, death was not to be the victor over what God had in store for them this day and, since life and death were in the hands of the Almighty alone, God breathed new life into

Pascale's body a His grace abound to him. From beneath Jorja's worn out body, life eclipsed death as Pascale came to and his body ejected the water from his lungs. And when he was breathing more easily, they gave glory to the One who had rescued and saved them both.

T he warm water lapped against their tired bodies as Jorja and Pascale drifted in the ocean some- where off the Abu Dhabi coast. Although grateful that God had spared them both, despair poked at their weary spirits and neither spoke of the dire position they now found themselves in. Instead, they silently pleaded that God would not only grant them the courage to finish what they had started, but that they would make it out alive.

In the cloudless sky above, the sun sat high and they clung to the wreckage in the sweltering heat, kicking their way toward the shoreline that grew more distant with each passing minute and was no longer within easy sight.

Time had become their enemy, and with most of the day already gone, they had made little to no progress in their fight against the current that seemed to push them farther away from their destination.

Weary and defeated, their energy soon dwindled and giving up seemed more inviting than their quest to get to shore. And so, when they were too tired to fight any longer, they submitted to nature and allowed the current to take them wherever it saw fit.

By the time they had just about given up hope, it had been more than twelve hours since their plane went down, and, as the day drew to a close and semi-darkness fell all around them, hope came when they least expected it.

With their bodies half-submerged, their hands still gripping onto the broken-off part of the airplane's wing, a hard jab to his ribs disrupted Pascale's sleep. Unable to ignore the persistent prods in his side, he eventually found the strength to lift and turn his head. At first he thought he was dreaming, but as his swollen, dry eyes adapted to the dusk light, there was no denying it. They had hit land.

"Jorja, wake up, we made it." His voice croaked as his one hand clutched at, then closed, over the sharp edges of a rock while the other still held onto the wreckage.

Jorja stirred and he called out to her again. This time, she lifted her head.

Pascale's face lit up against the rocky backdrop. "We made it," he smiled, and tugged at her arm until she was fully awake.

Dehydration had robbed her from having tears to run down her sun-beaten cheeks. Instead, she let go and allowed her body to slip off their make-shift raft. Crawling their way up and away from the water, they pulled themselves onto the rocks, pausing briefly to gain their bearings while Pascale rested his injured shoulder.

"Any idea where we are?" Jorja asked.

"Not yet, but we should keep our heads down for now. For all we know we're in Iran."

Pascale's eyes trailed the wall of rocks that ran in both directions alongside them then climbed to the top where it suddenly hit a low concrete wall.

"It's a port," he announced and dropped back against the rocks as soon as Jorja reached his side.

"Which means we have a ticket to the airport where a qualified pilot might actually get us to Italy." She smiled as she said it.

"About that," Pascale glanced at her reaction before he continued. "Our passports went down with the plane. It was in the bag I had stashed behind the wall in the hangar kitchen. And since it's fair to say I can't turn to my colleagues for help, I'm out of a backup plan."

"What about the flash drive and Diego's phone?"

He dropped his eyes to his belly. "They're in my belt bag but I doubt they would have survived the salty water."

Jorja drew quiet for the briefest of moments before she said, "If we can get to a phone I might be able to get us new passports. Don't ask," she quickly added when Pascale cast a concerned glance her way.

Leaning back against the rocks, he threw his hands in the air as if to say he'd rather not know, then peered over the edge of the wall. A moment later he hoisted himself over before turning back to help Jorja.

With darkness now their ally, they sneaked along the port wall toward the harbor where they hid between several stacked shipping containers. Under the faint boatyard lights, Pascale searched through the Arabic markings on the containers and soon learned where they had washed up.

"I think we're in Dubai," he said as his face scrunched in a curious frown.

"You sure?"

"It's written all over these containers."

"Who ever said miracles don't exist? If we can find a way to the airport we're only a six-hour flight away from Venice. We can still do this, Pascale."

"We have no choice do we? Not when the entire world has turned against us."

She touched his face. "We're going to be fine. Nothing we haven't done before, right?"

With obvious signs of pain and discomfort, Pascale smiled back bravely. "Let's get you to make that call then, shall we?"

He peered across the nearby shipyard and spotted a faint light a little further up.

"Over there, that must be the harbor master's office." He pointed to it with his chin.

"Right behind you," Jorja said.

They darted between the rows of containers then across a small clearing to a nearby building that seemed closed for the night. Glancing back and around, they moved in the direction of the lights, narrowly missing two shipping crew members where they came off a large parked vessel's gang-plank. When the men had passed and they were certain there wasn't anyone else following them, they escaped from behind the giant pile of shipping ropes they had hidden behind and ran the final stretch toward the small building.

A brief glance into a nearby window on the side of the building showed that there was a man sitting behind a large wooden desk poring over several maps and papers in front of him. On one end of the desk, his cellphone lay nearly completely buried under the pile of papers.

"Looks like he's alone," Pascale said.

"We're going to need a distraction if we want to get hold of that phone," Jorja quickly added.

"Any ideas?"

"Only the oldest trick in the book."

When a silent exchange told each other that they were ready to make their move, Jorja took a deep breath and set her plan in motion.

Storming into the port master's office, she charged toward him and frantically cried out for his help as if she were in distress. The scrawny Arab jumped up and hastily pushed back his chair. Then, just as quickly, he rushed towards her when she pretended to faint. When he reached out to catch her, she rotated his shoulders to get behind him then wrapped her arm in a choke hold around his neck. Moments later, the innocent man's body went limp and fell to her feet.

"A sleeper choke; impressive," Pascale said as he entered and shut the door behind them. "I didn't know you had martial arts training."

"I ran a few classes back in the day." She was already behind the desk searching for the cellphone through the messy desk.

"Got it!" she said as she climbed over the harbor master and handed it to Pascale, then bent down to roll the man over. "I'll hold his head while you scan his face to unlock it," she said.

The cellphone unlocked instantly and Pascale scrolled his thumb across the screen. "There, I've changed it to English and removed the location tracking. You also won't need to enter a passcode again to unlock it. Sorry, my friend," Pascale apologized over his shoulder as they climbed over the sleeping body and charged out of the office.

But when Jorja moved toward a dirty white sedan that stood parked nearby, Pascale grabbed hold of her arm to pull her back. "Where are you going? He's not going to stay asleep forever. We need to get out of here."

Jorja smiled and held up her hand from which a set of keys dangled from her index finger.

"I know, which is why we're borrowing his car," she said, smiling as she tossed the keys to Pascale and walked around the car to get in. When he slipped in behind the wheel and started the engine, she was already on the phone.

"Hey, Andre, it's Georgina."

"Dang, woman! You're like a cat with nine lives. Where you at, fam? Your face is all over the box. What you go doing now, huh?"

Jorja shuffled upright in her seat and pressed the phone closer to her ear. "What do you mean my face is all over the television?"

"Interpol, feds, all them coppers, they're all after you, bruv. You and them copper snitch."

"Is that what they're saying? They're saying he turned on them?"

"Yeah, fam, there's a bounty out too. We're talking serious dosh for the pair of you."

"How much? Actually, it doesn't matter. I need your help, Andre. We need passports and tickets for the next flight out of Dubai. We're making our way to the airport now so the sooner the better. I promise I'll make it up to you."

Mad Dog let out a whistle. "Dubai? You're going to get yourself locked up in one of them Arab slave prisons, Gigi. Have I not taught you anything, huh?"

"I did it for Ben, Andre. He finally has the life he's always wanted."

"And you gave up yours. And now you're running away with a bent cop."

"I did what I had to, Andre, and he's not a crooked cop. He's being set up." She looked away, aware that Pascale had glanced at her. "I need your help, Andre, please." Her voice was fragile and pleading.

"You know I'll do anything for you, Gigi, but you're in deep this time."

"I know, and I'm sorry. I have no one else to turn to."

She heard as Andre loudly sucked back on his teeth in reluctant surrender.

"I know a guy. One of them sleazy backstreet guys who hangs out near the souks and cheats the tourists. But he owes me and he's jacked. I'll have him meet you at the airport. Where are you heading?"

"Venice, Italy."

"Consider it done. Ditch this phone and text me from a burner when you're there."

"Thank you, Andre. I owe you."

"Just promise me you'll come home alive, Gigi."

But it was a promise Jorja didn't know if she could keep, and she ended the call with a simple goodbye instead.

CHAPTER EIGHTEEN

Having wiped and disposed of the port master's cellphone, Jorja and Pascale drove the short fifteen-minute distance to Dubai International Airport.

"I appreciate what you did back there," Pascale said as they reached the halfway mark to the airport. "I haven't had many people in my life who would stand up for me like that."

"I only told the truth."

"Well, it means a lot." He paused and pressed his lips together as if to choose his words wisely before he spoke again. "It must be nice to have friends you can rely on, but are you sure we can trust this Andre friend of yours?"

Jorja scoffed. "With my life. I've known him since I was just a kid. He's taught me most of what I know to survive on the streets. If you trust me, you can trust him."

"Fair enough. What about the guy we're supposed to meet at the airport?"

"I don't know him, but Andre's one Jamaican you don't want to cross, believe me. Whoever he has in his back pocket will come through for us, I'm sure."

"Let's hope you're right. Not to be cynical or anything but I thought I had trustworthy friends too. Turns out they didn't think twice about stabbing me in the back."

"I'm sorry that happened to you, Pascale, but not all your friends are untrustworthy."

He gave her a sideways glance. "So we're friends now, are we?"

She blushed, sidestepping his question when she abruptly told him to stop and pull over at an approaching corner shop.

Pascale frowned with confusion. "Sorry, I didn't mean to push the boundaries. I am very okay with being your friend right now. Heaven knows I need one." He slowed down and pulled the car into a nearby parking spot along the side of the road.

But Jorja's mind was already elsewhere when she said, "You didn't, it's fine. Just keep the car running. I'll be back in a minute," then hastily got out of the car and headed into the shop.

A few short minutes later, she was back. "Go, go, go!" she yelled when she was barely in her seat.

Pascale flattened the accelerator, nearly cutting a car off as he veered into the traffic and over onto the far lane.

"Why do I feel like I'm suddenly the getaway driver in a bank heist?" he asked, as he took the next turn towards the airport terminal.

"Because, you are." She pulled several items of clothing out from under her shirt and Pascale shifted uncomfortably in his seat.

"Look, I don't like this any more than you do and I can only hope that God forgives me for committing yet again another sin, but we will never make it onto the plane looking like this." She tugged, annoyed, at her dirty t-shirt that had ripped along the bottom during the plane crash.

Pascale smiled. "You're right, I'm sorry. I didn't even think of changing our clothes. I just wish there was another way."

"I know," she replied because, in truth, there was nothing more she could say or do that would rid her of the rotten feeling she now had inside. And, by the time Pascale had parked the car in the crowded airport parking, guilt had left its mark on Jorja's soul and her heart was once again heavy with regret and self-condemnation.

"You go first," Pascale said as he turned his back to her and covered his face with his hands.

Welcoming the brief moment of privacy, she quickly slipped into a navy t-shirt and covered it with a white linen long sleeve shirt before wrapping a matching white linen scarf around her neck.

"Thanks, I'm done." She dropped a gray tunic on his lap and turned her back in turn.

While Pascale changed, she picked up the disposable phone, which she had swiped from the shop too and quickly set about sending Andre a text message to say they had arrived.

Barely a few minutes later, a message with a meeting point came back.

"We're on," she announced and straightened her hair before scooping up their clothes.

"We should wipe our prints," Pascale said when she opened the door to get out.

When they were satisfied they hadn't left any traces behind, they dumped their clothing in the nearby trashcan and walked into the crowded terminal.

I t was easy to blend in with the bustling passengers as they went in search of the coffee shop where they were meant to wait for Andre's contact. They kept their heads down, making sure not to be caught on the vast network of surveillance cameras that laced the airport.

Having easily found the coffee shop, they took a seat at one of the tables that stood along the outer edges of the café and opened to the rest of the terminal.

"Shouldn't we sit closer to the back where no one can see us as easily?" Pascale queried when Jorja shuffled into her chair.

"You're thinking too much like an Interpol agent." She smiled mischievously, inviting an obscured chuckle from him in return.

"I guess, since I've crossed to the other side, you'll have to teach me how it's done then."

She shuffled uncomfortably.

"Sorry, I wasn't thinking," he apologized. "I just meant—"

"I know what you meant, Pascale. Once a thief, always a thief, right?"

"You're wrong. That's not what I meant at all."

"Yet here I am, forced back into the life I just can't seem to escape. Let's face it, Pascale, I'll never be anything other than a criminal in your eyes, so it really doesn't matter how you're trying to sugarcoat your true opinion of me right now. We are on opposite sides of the law and you will do whatever it takes to take down criminals like me, even if that means using me to do it for you. So, let's just agree to get this done and we never have to see each other ever again. Okay?"

He reached across the table to touch her hand but she pulled away.

"No, it's not okay," he said regardless. "I don't think of you as a criminal. I never have. Even that first night when I saw you in that little church in Geneva, you intrigued me. And when I watched you steal the *Salvator Mundi*, I had nothing but admiration and respect for you. I was quite prepared to let you go back to your life in St. Ives. None of this turned out the way it was supposed to. But my orders came from above, and now I know why. It was all orchestrated to get us to do Diego's dirty work for him. We were both used, Jorja. Heck, my own people nearly killed me yesterday." His voice cracked as he spoke and he quickly looked away.

Jorja was about to say something when a young Arab man knocked his chair against hers as he sat down behind her.

"So sorry, Miss," he said, but his eyes conveyed a different message before he sat down at his table, his back facing hers.

"What I wouldn't do for a cup of English tea right now," she said as she pretended to read the menu.

Pascale looked at her with confusion over her random comment that didn't fit with their conversation. But Jorja's eyes flashed at him over the rim of her menu and instantly told him that their clandestine meeting had already begun.

Moments later a waiter placed a serving tray with a pot of tea, two cups, and a container filled with sachets of sugar in front of them then, walked away.

Jorja reached into the sugar dish and thumbed her way to the only sachet that had been placed upside down. She slipped it inside her sleeve then took another and added it to her cup. Behind her, the Arab man got up and quickly disappeared between the passersby.

"Was that him? Shouldn't we follow him somewhere?" Pascale whispered across the table as he watched her pour tea into their cups.

"Drink up," she said from behind her cup and gulped its contents down.

Realizing he was at a loss over a process he seemingly had no intel on, he drained his cup.

Having quickly scanned the sugar sachet earlier before she tucked it up her sleeve, Jorja led them through the busy terminal according to the short cryptic directions that were left on the packet. When they reached a wall of upright public storage lockers, she tore open the sugar packet and took out the key, shielding the action with her body.

Pascale watched in awe of the skillfully executed plan, once again impressed by her ingenuity and precision as she moved to retrieve a pink leopard-print carry-on.

"Can't say it suits you," Pascale teased when she pulled out the handle to wheel it away.

She smiled, forgetting briefly of their earlier spat. "It's Andre's idea of a joke. His entire apartment looks like this."

"I'd love to meet this guy one day, but where do we go to get the passports done?"

Again, she giggled. "It has already been done."

"Wait, what? How?"

She reached inside the bag's outer pocket and pulled out two Italian passports then scanned through his.

"How's your Italian, Luigi?"

She pressed the passport to his chest and flashed an amused smile at him.

"Luigi? Like the cartoon character? Is this some kind of Jamaican joke too? Are you seriously telling me your clever friend couldn't come up with something a bit more original? And where did he get this photo? It looks nothing like me."

Jorja began to walk away, dragging the suitcase behind her as Pascale scurried alongside her.

"Not yet, but it will." She stopped then nudged her chin towards the elevator on the far end. "See that over there? We're going to step inside as Jorja and Pascale, but, when the doors open to the VIP lounge on the top floor, we'll be stepping out as Sophia and Luigi."

The next flight out of Dubai wasn't until early morning so, with disguises and counterfeit travel documents in place, Jorja and Pascale waited until then to board the first flight to Venice, Italy. And, true to his word, Andre managed to get them safely out of the Emirates. Mere hours later, the pair stepped out onto Italian soil where newfound hope and the prospects of soon putting it all behind them lay in wait.

But it wasn't all that was waiting for them.

CHAPTER NINETEEN

The gun pressed into Jorja's ribcage the moment she stepped out of the terminal at Marco Polo Airport. Soon after, a second assailant pressed himself up against Pascale whose large hand closed firmly around his injured arm. Pascale flinched but the man ignored him and spitefully tightened his grip.

"Walk," one of the men commanded them.

Recognizing the two men from the night they met with Diego, Jorja and Pascale didn't argue and willingly walked with them toward a white limo that stood parked on the opposite side of the road. When they stepped inside, Diego's grim face greeted them where they had settled into the seat opposite him. Pascale's back stiffened as he waited for Diego to speak but instead, Diego's eyes narrowed as he examined the pair.

It was Jorja who spoke first. "The flash drive. You've been tracking us, haven't you?"

Diego's face relaxed into a slight close-lipped smile.

"I'm impressed, Miss Rose."

So was Pascale, evident in the way he now watched the silent stand-down play off between Jorja and Diego. When neither of them said anything else, Pascale decided to take back control of the situation.

"What do you want, Diego?"

Diego's eyes pinned on Pascale's face. "I'm just making sure my assets are intact."

"And by assets you mean what, exactly, us or your paintings?" Pascale probed.

Diego gave a throaty chuckle. "Both, really. I heard your own people want you dead. Five million apiece is nothing to scorn at."

He paused as the information of their bounty left both Jorja and Pascale rigid and staring back at him with wide eyes. "Don't worry, I don't plan on handing you over to the Feds. Even combined the money is worth far less to me than the three paintings."

"But you've come to finish the job yourself, right? Since we're hot targets that might expose you and the locations of those paintings. So now you need to kill us before they do. I get it. We don't trust you either." Pascale's voice was loaded with accusation.

Diego leaned forward, his scarred cheeks rising every few seconds as the muscles in his jaw tightened and released.

"If I wanted to kill you, Pascale, you'd be dead already. But what good would that do me? I told you, those paintings are worth far more to me than the price tags on your heads. I'm not an unreasonable man. I just want what's mine. And you're wrong, by the way. I told you from the beginning, trust is everything in my line of business. If you wanted to do me one over, you'd have done it by now. You have as much riding on this as I do. Your colleagues somehow think you're playing both sides of the fence. Your honor is at stake and proving your innocence is the only way you'll keep it."

"If you trust us, why this meeting?" Jorja broke the tension.

"Because, unfortunately, the circumstances have changed, and not only do you now have a target on your back that, yes, could expose me, I am now also at risk of losing valuable business." He sat back and lit a cigar. "I've come to tell you that we're running out of time. You have three days to bring me those paintings or the next time I see you, you'll wish you were dead instead."

Shock settled on Jorja's face. "Three days! That's impossible. We need time to prepare, scope out the premises. We need money, equipment, it can't be done." She crossed her arms.

But the throbbing veins in Diego's tanned neck told them there was no room for any negotiations.

"Three days," Diego repeated as his eyes flashed to his black-suited henchman who sat next to him.

Promptly, the man climbed out and held the door for Jorja and Pascale to step out of the car. Once they had, he placed a tan rucksack next to their feet and turned to get back into the car.

When Diego's car drove off, Pascale's hands went to his hips where he paced a small circle in front of Jorja. "We need to get out of here. Five million a piece! That's enough to get the entire world coming after us. No wonder he only gave us three days to get those paintings. Every day beyond that is a day closer to us getting found." Suddenly feeling exposed, his eyes flashed into all directions, scanning the surrounds for any threats. Without letting another moment pass by, he scooped up the bag by his feet and headed toward the nearby water's edge, briefly looking back at Jorja to follow him where she hadn't moved or said a word since Diego's car drove away.

"Jorja, are you listening to me? We need to get out of here. If we can find a boat we can get across to San Marco in half the time."

But Jorja's dead gaze into the distance told him her mind was elsewhere occupied.

He flung the rucksack over his shoulder and grabbed hold of her hand, dragging her behind him as he made toward the water's edge.

"It doesn't make sense," Jorja said as she pulled away from him and stopped.

"What doesn't?"

"Diego didn't turn your team against you. If he was the one pulling Interpol's strings he would have killed us here and now. He didn't."

"That's because he's greedy. He said it himself. The bounty is worth less than the paintings."

"It's still a lot of money, Pascale. I think he's telling the truth. He's not the one pulling the strings. Besides, he needs us. Putting an order out for us to be killed won't get him what he wants. He's after those paintings, not the money, and certainly not your honor. I think he was here to make sure we were safe, to help us."

Pascale turned to face Jorja head-on. "And what makes you think he won't hand us over and collect the bounty once he has those paintings, Jorja? A man like that doesn't let his victims go. We know too much. He will kill us before he makes true on his empty promises to us. You can't trust Diego Cortez. He's in this for himself, nothing and no one else but himself. Now, let's get out of here before someone else beats him to it. Once we have the paintings we'll figure out a way to get out of this, even if it means we have to resort to killing him."

But Jorja's intuition told her differently and she pulled at the tan backpack on Pascale's shoulder.

"I think you're wrong. We can trust him. I bet you every-thing I have left that whatever's inside this bag will help us get those paintings."

Pascale's stunned face told her he disagreed. But, in his eyes there was also no denying that a part of him was desperate to believe her and that he hadn't even thought of looking inside the bag. When he didn't say or react, she gently pulled at the strap to take it from him.

Pascale let it slide off his shoulder and watched as she unclipped the fastener to peek inside.

"And?" he said. "What's inside?"

She smiled and snapped the clasp back in place.

"It's not a bomb if that's what you were thinking." She handed the satchel back to him and added, "It's a bag full of everything we might need to get the job done. I told you, the guy is on our side, Pascale."

Pascale tossed it back over his shoulder. "Let's hope it stays that way. For all we know he might be leading us straight into a trap. Either way, I choose to trust your instincts, so can we please get out of here before we get a bullet in our backs from the people we know are definitely out to kill us? I feel like the world's eyes are suddenly upon us."

Jorja nodded in agreement and followed him down toward the water's edge where he had earlier spotted a sign directing them to the water taxis. Once there, an athletically built skipper with a small speedboat pulled up to them and offered to take them across. The choice seemed obvious since it appeared the fit skipper would more easily be able to handle any challenges that might come their way.

With newfound trust pinned on an enemy who seemingly turned into an ally, they hopped onboard and instructed him to deliver them to San Polo where the *Scuola Grande Di San Rocco* would be their first target.

As they settled into the white leather seating of the boat and headed out across the water, Pascale noticed the smeared bloody patch on the floorboard next to them.

CHAPTER TWENTY

The boat glided across the canal, increasing speed as it pushed further away from the shoreline. Pascale's eyes remained pinned on the bloodstain at his feet while his mind raced to find a logical reason for it being there. It could have simply been a previous passenger's nosebleed, or a cut on someone's finger. But no matter how hard he tried to find a logical explanation for its existence, dread had already taken over his insides. So too did his flesh instinctively react when every muscle in his body suddenly went taut with suspicion. His eyes searched over the surfaces, hoping that his instincts were acting on paranoia instead of what it was telling him. But it wasn't long before he found two more droplets of fresh blood against the back of the steersman's chair. He glanced to his left where Jorja's eyes had spotted it too. A slight raise of her eyebrow told him her instincts were in agreement with his. The man steering them away from the shore was an imposter and he must have killed the real skipper when he hijacked the boat. As they silently weighed up their options, all they could do now was be ready. While they played into their kidnapper's game and prayed that they were both wrong, they remained still, waiting, expecting trouble.

And, when roughly halfway into their trip the skipper suddenly cut the boat's engine and turned a gun on them, their suspicions were confirmed.

The young man's tanned skin glistened with sweat under the Venetian sun, his dark eyes now fixed on his targets. As he steadied his footing in the boat when the choppy water swayed it to and fro, the tip of his gun wagged confidently toward them to raise their hands.

They did as he instructed.

The man approached Pascale first—assuming he was the biggest threat. Cable ties in hand he told Pascale to slip one around his wrists while his gun tipped back and forth between their heads.

"You're making a mistake," Pascale tried to reason.

The man chuckled. "Well, then I guess my mistake is going to make me a very rich man when I bring the pair of you in and collect my bounty."

"How did you find us?" Jorja asked as Pascale proceeded to slip the cable tie over his hands.

"Wouldn't you like to know," he said mockingly before he used his free hand to pull the tie tight around Pascale's wrists. As he turned to instruct Jorja to do the same, he squatted in front of her, his face smug with victory when he decided to answer her anyway. "Show me a crooked man who'd say no to a small cut in exchange for a little bit of information. That much money is more than he makes in a lifetime cheating his way through the souks. Now, quit messing around and put this on."

He tossed the cable tie at her lap and rose to his feet, pointing the gun at Jorja's face.

"You don't know what you're getting yourself involved with," Pascale tried again.

"I don't really care, stupid. Now, shut up or I'll shut your mouth for you!"

"You should listen to him," Jorja said as she intentionally fumbled with the cable tie.

He bellowed a sarcastic laugh before his face turned serious. "I don't take orders from a woman. Especially one who can't even follow a simple instruction."

He squat down again and yanked the cable tie from her hand. With the gun now tucked inside his waistband, he used both hands and proceeded to slip the plastic tether over Jorja's hands.

It was the moment she had been baiting him for.

In one swift movement Jorja thrust her head forward, headbutting him in his nose. The man fell back and groaned in pain as the impact of her defense rendered his nose broken and bleeding. As he squirmed to get back on his feet, the gun now gripped in his hand as he scrambled to get into position to take aim, Pascale leaned back in his seat and kicked it from his hand. The gun slid across the small deck as the skipper lunged forward to take a punch at Jorja. She ducked, delivering in turn a punch of her own that slammed into her attacker's ribs. He clutched at his side, bending at the waist. Seizing her opponent's vulnerability, Jorja delivered an uppercut to his jaw that left him stumbling back into the driver's seat. But he was a hard one to knock out and was quick to retaliate with a punch of his own. Once more Jorja ducked and missed his fist, following through with a left hook that knocked him onto the floor next to his gun. Pascale leapt to where the gun had wedged itself into one of the corners, fighting to get to it first. As the two men wrestled on the floor, a single gunshot rang through the air before all motion seized.

Jorja's blood ran cold in anticipation of Pascale being the one who got shot. For a brief moment her legs were stuck to the floor, unable to move as she waited. There was a groan, then movement of the skipper's arm where he and Pascale's bodies were entangled on the floor.

"Pascale," she called out with a wavering voice but got no reply.

Dread filled her body with fear.

Her heart thumped loudly in her chest.

Then the limp body of the skipper rolled off to one side.

"Pascale!" she yelled as she caught sight of the large blood-soaked patch on his chest.

When he didn't answer she yanked the skipper by the arm and pulled him to one side, checking briefly over her shoulder if he was still alive.

But he wasn't.

Her hands moved to Pascale's blood-drenched abdomen and pulled his shirt away in search of a wound.

"I'm fine," he groaned as he held up the gun in his bound hands.

Jorja pulled him upright, remaining hunched down as she glanced over the side of the boat for the first time. There was no one around.

"I don't think anyone saw or heard anything but we should get out of here."

She helped Pascale to his feet and once again went for the multitool to cut the cable tie.

"That was quite the fight you delivered. This guy didn't have an inkling of who he was up against," he chuckled.

"I did warn him, didn't I?" She smiled back.

"If only he had listened then he'd still be alive right now and we wouldn't be stuck with a dead body onboard. He can't stay here. We're going to have to throw him overboard. We need this boat. Take his feet. I'll take the heavy side."

But when Jorja didn't react and instead stood staring at the corpse on the floor, he stopped and took her hands in his.

"It was an accident, Jorja. Self defense, if you will."

"That doesn't make it right. We killed this man, Pascale. I didn't sign up for any of this. Yes, I was once a thief, but I have never killed anyone, ever. And now look at me. I'm a liar, a thief, and an accomplice to murder. Just one more hefty sin in a long list of black-stained wickedness."

"I know. I am as guilty as you are and I wish with all my heart I could go back and change things. But all I know right now is that we have a target on our backs and if this guy got Andre's trusty associate in Dubai to sing so easily, there are more coming for us, not forgetting the fact that my backstabbing team is also still out there somewhere. The quicker we get those paintings, the quicker we can disappear and put all of this behind us. And believe me, I want nothing more than to figure out what the connection is between Gerard and Diego. Trust me, I'm going to get to the bottom of this and take the whole lot of them down. With or without my bureau's help. It's going to work out, I promise." His eyes searched hers.

"Okay," she whispered.

Pascale gently squeezed her hands before they slipped the bounty hunter's body overboard and watched it sink deeper into the choppy water. Soaking up the blood with Pascale's already-stained shirt, they washed the red fluid off the floor and hid the item of clothing in a compartment under one of the seats. If all went according to plan, they would be in Rome for the next heist by the time the authorities discovered the abandoned boat in one of the canals.

"What do you say we get out of here and onto dry land? I think I've had enough of water that's fraught with danger," Pascale said, already gliding the boat toward land.

"You do know Venice is built on water, don't you?"

"Like I said, the sooner we get this done the better."

"Aye aye, captain," she said with a mocking salute and sank back into the chair next to him.

CHAPTER TWENTY-ONE

P ascale navigated the boat through the narrow Venice canals. The map Jorja found amongst the various tools and gadgets in the satchel Diego gave them, delivered them to a small mooring close to the *Scuola Grande di San Rocco*.

Where Jorja sat poring over the bag of tools in her lap, she found herself apprehensive to proceed, and for the first time in her life, she fought the urge to go through with the job. It was as if every instinct in her body told her to run. As far away from everything as humanly possible. But whilst it would be fairly easy to disappear between the narrow canal-side streets of Venice, the feasibility thereof was far more daunting. She couldn't run even if she wanted to. She had nowhere to go. Going back to St. Ives wasn't an option—it would be the first place they'd come looking for her—be it Diego, Interpol, or Pascale. It was as if she was stuck in limbo between two lifetimes, a cross-roads with neither path being an option. Her life was in ruins, her soul distraught with guilt that she feared could never be atoned for.

She shut her eyes for a brief moment, her back turned toward Pascale where he was focused on parking the boat, and she shared her heart with the only One who truly knew her. Vulnerable and filled with a lifetime of regrets, she wished she could turn back time and start all over again. How different her life would have been if she had never met Ben, never chose to steal, never got involved with the likes of Gustav Züber. Perhaps she would have had that Art degree her father always nagged her about. She could have been taking care of the art, enjoyed each piece instead of stealing and selling them off into the criminal underground.

But she had made her choices and there was no time left for remorse.

She inhaled deeply, held it for a brief moment, then exhaled slowly as she opened her eyes again.

"I'm ready," she announced with a heavy heart when Pascale came to stand in front of her.

"You sure? Why do I feel like something's up?" He plonked himself down in the seat next to her. "We can't afford to mess this up Jorja so, if there's something on your mind, tell me. We're going to need our wits about us."

"I'm fine, just eager to move on, that's all."

"I hear you. So let's get this show on the road, shall we?" He pointed to a spot on the map. "There's a café directly opposite the *Scuola*. I say we use that as our stakeout post."

"No, there's no time for surveillance. We'll have to go in as tourists and improvise from there. According to this brochure, the next tour starts in fifteen minutes."

"I'll follow your lead."

Jorja handed him an in-ear communication device and popped the second one into her left ear. "Testing, testing, one, two, three."

"Soundcheck clear," Pascale replied as he pulled on the dead skipper's baseball cap and dropped the bill lower over his eyes.

"Let's do this," he said as they stepped off the boat and set off along the sand-colored cobbled streets that weaved between the large square buildings.

Less than ten minutes later they fell in line with a small group of tourists who stood waiting on the steps of the *Scuola*. Before long, the pair entered the historical building.

It was easy to blend in with the crowd as they moved through the vast rectangular hall where two rows of columns divided the side aisles that led up to a nave.

"I don't see it," Pascale announced after he studied the eight large Tintoretto canvases on the wall that showed episodes from the life of the Virgin Mary and Christ's childhood.

"You won't. A stolen painting with this much heat won't be hanging on the walls for all to see. It will be stored away, hidden somewhere to be retrieved when the need arises. We're looking for a smaller room like an archive. Something the public won't have access to."

When neither saw anything that might fit the criteria, they followed the guided tour upstairs to the Chapter Room where several more Biblical scenes painted by Tintoretto adorned the entire ceiling.

"Nothing," Pascale whispered.

From where they stood, Jorja tore her attention away from the spellbinding depictions above her head and, out one of the large windows, spotted the small steeple of a church that stood adjacent to the *Scuolo*. She moved to the window to grab a closer look. Pascale followed her.

"I think we've found our mark," she whispered as she carefully motioned towards the nearby church building.

"How can you tell?"

"Just a hunch."

"Are you sure? According to Diego the painting is somewhere inside this building. That church isn't even attached to this building, it's on the other side of the canal." He peered at the waterway below that divided the two buildings.

"It's the *Church of Saint Roch,* named after the saint who initiated the San Rocco fraternity. According to this brochure, this entire building's existence was because of him. So much so that his remains have been in the possession of the San Rocco brotherhood since 1485. Trust me, it's there."

They bided their time and when it was safe for them to sneak out without causing suspicion, they made their exit.

When they crossed the small pedestrian bridge that stretched over the narrow canal below, Pascale glanced sideways and saw that, from their stance, their boat was in full view in the nearby waterway.

Pascale jolted to a sudden halt and took a step back to have a closer look.

"They found it! They found the boat, Jorja," he said as he watched the small team of policemen who had gathered next to it. Two more policemen were already searching the boat and Pascale knew it wouldn't be long before they found his bloody shirt.

Jorja tugged him by the arm to keep moving.

"It's fine, we'll find another way to get to Rome. It will take a while before they tie us to the boat and come looking for us anyway and by the time they track us down, we'll be long gone."

Determined to find the painting, another obstacle soon caught them off guard. Unaware of the renovations that were underway at the church, they found the large wooden doors of the church locked and closed off to the public.

"Perhaps there's a side entrance somewhere," Pascale suggested when the nearby street vendors posed it too risky to pick the lock in broad daylight.

"This way," he motioned and led Jorja toward the narrow alleyway that ran between the church and a large building next to it. Resembling a very narrow passage that was entirely cast in the dark shadows of the two flanking build-ings, it provided the perfect amount of obscurity and it wasn't long before they discovered a small door to the side of the church.

"I'll keep watch while you take a crack at picking the lock," Pascale said after an elderly woman squeezed past them and soon left out the other end of the narrow lane.

When the coast was clear, Jorja set about forcing open the lock and in no time she succeeded.

"Got it," she announced, giving one more quick check for any passersby before they sneaked inside the church.

An awe-inspiring gilded pulpit glistened in the light that came from the overhead semi-dome's ornate windows, illuminating the entire church around them. Tintoretto's paintings adorned the expansive roof of the apse, giving it an atmosphere similar to that inside Michelangelo's Sistine Chapel. On each of the sweeping walls, more paintings left them mesmerized and had them take a brief pause to soak it all in.

"I don't think I've ever seen anything as beautiful," Jorja said.

"Me neither. At some point in the near future we will have to come back here but for now, we have to find *Rembrandt's Sea of Galilee,* before we end up not having a future at all. Any idea where to start looking?"

Jorja stood in the center of the church and quietly scanned her eyes over the interior.

"Did you hear me? We don't have time to admire the artistry, Jorja, we have to get going."

Still she didn't answer and Pascale watched as she then moved to stop in front of one the walls directly below the organ loft. Her palms glided across the decorative etchings, lightly touching and feeling each carving. Following the wall, she traced the textured surface with her fingertips until she suddenly stopped, pausing her hand over a spot in the wall.

CHAPTER TWENTY-TWO

Her actions had Pascale curious and he hurried over to join her.

"What's happening?" he whispered, conscious not to interrupt her trance-like state where she now stood with her cheek flush against the wall, while her fingers lightly tapped at the textured surface.

"I think we may have found what we're looking for."

"We did? All I see are etchings and a giant organ above us."

Excitement broke on Jorja's face. "Oh, it's here all right. Come, follow me."

She beckoned for Pascale to follow her as she darted to the spiral wooden staircase that led up to the organ loft. The ornate organ towered above them, flanked by columns and angel statuettes playing harps and violins.

"I'm sorry but I still don't see it," Pascale said, his hands now on his hips as he skimmed over the statues.

With her full attention now aimed at the large silver organ pipes that stretched up behind the organ keys, Jorja let her hands rest on the keys for a brief moment before they drifted up to the round pushbutton switches.

"I can tell you're doing some weird thief-thing, Jorja, but please enlighten me so I don't lose my mind over here."

A light frown broke on her forehead, her mind still otherwise occupied as she mumbled under her breath. "They are all accounted for."

Pascale hovered over her shoulder.

"What, the pistons?" he said, more confused than ever.

"Yes, I was so sure they were..."

"Were what?" Pascale's patience was wearing thin with Jorja's reticence but as he was about to make his frustration known, he watched her drop onto her hands and knees below the organ.

Reaching out to one of the toe studs, she pushed down on it. The floor creaked somewhere to their right and she crawled on all fours over to where a large split now ran through the mahogany floor. Her fingers trailed the crack in the floorboards to where it stopped at the edge of a loose tapestry rug.

"Here!" she exclaimed and flipped the thin rug over to one side.

Underneath the loose mat, her fingers traced a solid brass flush ring handle and she immediately pulled at it. A meter squared trapdoor opened in the wooden floor.

"I'm speechless. How did you... I mean, of all the places to look in this church, and you somehow knew to look here?" Pascale remarked.

"I told you, you have to put yourself in the mind of a thief. Come on!" she hurried him to follow her down a set of small wooden steps into the concealed room directly underneath the organ.

The tiny low-bearing room was dark and a strong odor of furniture oil lay thick in the condensed air. Under torch-light, a small pile of spare organ pipes lay covered under a cloth tarp in one corner, next to it, a wooden crate with a few tools and a half-open tin of wood floor wax. On the other end of the room, a narrow cavity in the roof stretched up into the organ pipes above, leaving the rest of the small room entirely empty.

"It's just the organ mechanics room," Pascale said with a dejected tone.

But Jorja wasn't convinced.

She peered up into the cavity, allowing her eyes to carefully inspect every metal pipe as she shone the flashlight up inside the hollow space of each one. A few minutes later, she looked back at Pascale, a wide grin flashing across her face.

"You're kidding," he said in awe.

"Nope, take this." She passed the flashlight to Pascale then wedged her torso between the pipes until her arm could reach up inside one of them. Groaning under the strain as she stretched deeper into the pipe, Jorja let out a frustrated sigh when her reach wasn't far enough.

"Let me try," Pascale offered and took over from her.

Jorja's heart thumped hard with excitement as she watched Pascale use his good arm to stretch deep into the pipe. When he took too long she nearly allowed the surge of excited adrenaline to shove him out of the way so she could try again but she held back and bit down on her bottom lip. Tremors ran through her body in anticipation of finding the infamous piece of art that had been missing for over three decades. But her glee was soon eclipsed by despair knowing that once again the painting would be lost to the criminal underworld.

As bitterness slowly threatened to take over her heart, Pascale suddenly emerged with a leather storage tube, groaning as he relaxed on the floor beside it.

"Allow me to give you the honor of unveiling what's inside, Miss Rose," he said with his usual charm.

Anxious to see what was inside, Jorja took a deep breath and slowly puffed it out, her eyes now filled with excitement as they locked with Pascale's.

"What are you waiting for, Jorja? Go on, open it."

Butterflies tugged at her insides as she undid the single black clasp on the tube and slowly pulled out the rolled-up canvas. Tossing the storage tube aside, she carefully unrolled the painted canvas and gently slipped the acid-free paper off both sides. As if of one body, they each drew in a sharp breath at the precise moment the flashlight illuminated the painting.

It was what they had come for: *The Storm on the Sea of Galilee*, painted by Rembrandt in 1633 and the first of the items needed to buy back their freedom from Diego Cortez.

But their moment of awe was short-lived when a door suddenly slammed from somewhere inside the church.

Jorja killed the flashlight. They paused and listened. Shuffling noises filled the dead silent church and echoed toward them.

"We need to get out of here," Pascale whispered as he started rolling up the canvas before popping it back into the container.

Knowing that every noise they made would echo through the church below, they slowly made their way up through the hatch, closing the door and returning the rug over it.

Jorja peered through the railing over the edge of the organ loft, then shrugged her shoulders when she didn't see anyone.

"Let's make a run for the alleyway," she whispered as they hung back beside the organ and peered toward the door they had entered the church with.

Pascale nodded in agreement and they proceeded down the spiral staircase that suddenly creaked more than before. They paused. Scanning between the pews, they waited a few more seconds then hurriedly descended the final few steps. Weaving their way between the rows of pillars, they darted between the pews toward the door.

"Hey!" A male voice surprised them as a short, plump Italian shouted from behind.

When they ignored him and kept going, he yelled out at them again as he started chasing after them.

But Jorja and Pascale were too fast for the portly man whom they assumed had to be the caretaker, and they quickly escaped into the dark shadows of the alley. Choosing not to run toward the canal, they turned the other way and headed in the opposite direction. Their feet echoed loudly on the narrow stone streets as they ran further away from the church and deeper into the center of San Polo. When they finally reached a secluded spot away from the nearby bustling markets, they stopped.

"We need to get out of Venice and fast," Pascale said while catching his breath. "Judging by how quick the police responded to finding the missing boat, I think it's fair to say that our chubby little friend back there is talking to them as we stand here and breathe."

"I agree. They'll be all over the waterways and most likely the airport soon too."

"That leaves going by car or by public transport."

"Hiring a car will expose us even more. There will be a paper trail Harry and the guys will pick up on instantly. And stealing a car isn't an option," Jorja added sternly.

"Fine, then we're left with going by train. The bus will take too long."

They spread the map open on the nearby building's wall.

"We're not far from the station," Pascale said.

Flinging the painting canister over one arm, Jorja followed Pascale as he led them toward the train terminal.

Once there, Jorja held back next to a vending machine while Pascale went ahead and bought two tickets, making sure his face was hidden from any overhead surveillance cameras.

The train wasn't due for another ten minutes and he joined Jorja at the vending machine. Using the spare time to dispense a few packets of biscotti and two cappuccinos, they waited.

From the corner of her eye, Jorja noticed a policeman on patrol and she hastily hid the storage container behind her leg. When the officer walked by and cast a watchful eye their way, Pascale nodded politely and casually took a sip of his coffee. At first, the policeman passed them but then he stopped and took a step back. He turned and faced Pascale. A slight frown settled between his eyes as he stared at the baseball cap on Pascale's head.

"You like them?" he asked Pascale.

Jorja's heart skipped several beats.

Pascale didn't answer—he had no idea what he was talking about.

The police officer spoke again.

"The Yankees, you like them?" His eyes darted to the logo on the cap.

"Oh, no, not really," Pascale responded.

"But you're wearing their hat."

"It was a gift from a friend," Pascale said, then diverted the question. "How about you? Do you like them?"

"Can't say that I do. I was just curious because I always see the American tourists wearing them. You're not American." He looked at Jorja, his eyes nearly catching the concealed container behind her leg.

CHAPTER TWENTY-THREE

Pascale was quick to divert the policeman's attention back to his hat.

"My friend is always traveling. I think he picked this hat because it's so typically American, you know?" Pascale smiled.

Jorja's heart skipped several more beats, careful not to have him see the painting.

The policeman nodded then smiled, seemingly satisfied with his answer when he said, "Maybe one day I'll go visit America for myself. To see what all the fuss is about."

"Me too," Pascale said and smiled.

"Have a safe trip then," the policeman added.

"Thank you, Officer. You have a good day too." Pascale replied, keeping his cool.

When the policeman was a fair bit away, Jorja finally felt as if she could breathe again.

"That was close, Pascale. Too close."

"I know." Pascale took the cap off his head and tossed it in the nearby trash can. "Our train should be here any minute. Perhaps it's time we ditch these disguises and find new ones when we get to Rome." He glanced down at the painting. "That too. We're going to need to find another way of carrying that around with us or keep it in a storage locker in Rome somewhere."

"I'm not letting it out of my sight, Pascale. This is the only leverage we have to win back our freedom. Besides, we can use it to transport the next two paintings. Less to carry around. And, if we can get hold of a large coat, it should fit neatly underneath."

"Fine, I see your point," Pascale agreed just as the train pulled up to the platform.

hen they were a fair bit out of Venice and en route to Rome, having done another quick surveillance of the train car, Pascale took his seat opposite Jorja again.

"And? Is there anyone suspicious hanging about since the last time you checked five minutes ago?" Jorja asked smiling mischievously.

"None I'm aware of, no."

Pascale seemed restless.

"Then why the fidgeting?" Jorja asked.

Pascale leaned in. "Don't you find it strange?"

"What?"

"That no one's found us yet? It's almost too easy."

Jorja's lips curled into a smile. "And that's bad why exactly?"

Pascale sat back in his seat. "I'm not sure but I've been doing this a very long time and I'm finding it really curious that Harry hasn't picked up our trail yet. I know how good he is."

"Perhaps he's not as good as you think. Or perhaps we're just better at it. Besides, as far as they're aware our plane went down. And even if they got the Coastguard involved, and they're all back there searching for us, they have most likely given up hope of finding us alive by now. Presumed dead, they'd have called off the search. As far as I'm concerned, the bounty hunter got lucky. He had no exit strategy planned at all and, if you think about it, had no way of knowing we'd be arriving on that plane. He just happened to be in the right place at the right time. Probably saw our faces on the TV or something and decided to take a chance."

Pascale rubbed at his forehead before his fingers pinched the space between his eyes.

"I suppose you're right. It's just, I can't shake this feeling that something bad is about to happen."

"Like what?"

"Getting caught stealing a painting from the Vatican, for one," Pascale scoffed.

"We're not going to get caught, okay? Anyway, I think I've already found a way in."

"You've already come up with a plan on how we're going to break into a highly secure city never mind the building."

"Yep, except technically, we're not going to break in. We're going to be invited in."

Pascale snickered. "You've lost me."

"The Isabella Stewart Gardner heist. We're going to do exactly the same."

Pascale threw back his head in disbelief. "You're insane, Jorja! This isn't the nineties anymore. Dressing as two police officers and walking into one of the most secure places in the world isn't going to fly in today's day and age. It will never work. And I'm pretty sure the Vatican Palace in its entire enormity is under the protection of a top-notch private security company. There would be no need for any police officials to enter the building."

"Who said anything about dressing as police officers?"

Pascale's eyes narrowed as his head tilted to one side.

"Look, even if we managed to get inside the building, the place is huge. There's no way of knowing where to even begin looking for Caravaggio's painting. It could literally be anywhere, Jorja." He paused briefly then continued. "I think we should call the whole thing off, negotiate with Diego."

"Negotiate! How? With what? He'll kill us, Pascale."

"This entire mission was doomed from the start, Jorja. It's impossible to do what he's asking of us. A heist of this magnitude requires months of careful planning and even then it's still a mammoth task. Even with the bag of tricks he gave us. But who am I to tell you this? You of all people should know the risks involved."

Jorja fell silent as she digested his words.

"What do you suggest we tell him then? He'll never agree to drop this. He said it himself; these paintings are more valuable to him than anything else. As much as I would like to agree with you, I don't think we have much of a choice, Pascale."

Pascale let out a grunting sound.

"You're right. He won't let us go." He paused then continued. "I just need a good plate of food and some sleep. I'm not thinking clearly."

"It's been a lot, I know. How's your arm?"

"As long as I don't have to swing from it, fine. Okay, talk to me. What's the most likely place for us to find this painting?"

Jorja leaned in.

"The vault."

"Nah, that's way too obvious and as far as I'm aware, there's nothing but centuries-old documents and books down there. Besides, the place will be crawling with scholars."

"I'm not talking about the secret repository that runs beneath Saint Peter's Basilica. I'm talking about the Pope's private vault, where he keeps his tiaras and rings."

Pascale shuffled upright. "He has a private vault? You know this for sure."

"I do. Back in the day, Ben and I used to fantasize about breaking into it. There was a time we nearly did, but he decided last minute that it was too risky."

"Oh, great. It was too risky back then even with Ben's tech savvy contributions yet now you think we can do it. Just great."

"I've done most of the reconnaissance back then so, half the prep work is already done."

"If you can remember the details, yes, but you're talking about information you gathered decades ago, Jorja. Besides, how do we even know it's in the Pope's vault and not in the museum's vault? Wouldn't it be more likely to be there? That's where I'd keep a stolen painting."

"That's where you're wrong though. It's not a stolen painting, remember? At least, not in the eyes of the Pope."

Pascale frowned, prompting Jorja to elaborate.

"Diego told us that Gustav Züber double-crossed him when he intercepted one of his consignments and then sold his paintings to several private collectors all over the world."

"You think he sold it to the Vatican."

"I do. Caravaggio's painting is a nativity of Jesus with St. Francis and St. Lawrence. Back in 1609 these two Roman priests were greatly revered, similar to how the world sees Pope Francis today. A historic piece of art like this holds special significance to the church and Gustav would have milked that opportunity. Trust me, it's in the Pope's private vault."

"Then surely if it's of that much sentimental value to the Pope he'd have it displayed somewhere instead."

"It is. His vault is a mini museum of sorts, set up for his personal enjoyment. They all have them. The Queen, the White House, private collectors, you name it. It's where they keep their personal jewelry, tiaras, royal ceremonial relics, journals, pretty much anything that has personal value to them."

Pascale stared out the small window as the train entered the outskirts of Rome.

"I'm too scared to ask but I'm going to anyway." He scratched at the back of his neck. "How exactly do you intend for us to get invited into this private treasury if the Pope's the only one who makes use of it?"

Jorja sat back and crossed her arms as a smile broke on her face.

"We're going to create just cause."

CHAPTER TWENTY-FOUR

They found a small, quiet hotel within walking distance of Saint Peter's Square where solitude from each other proved more needed than either of them had anticipated.

When morning came around, Jorja met Pascale in the lobby.

"You look like you hadn't slept a wink all night," she said to Pascale when she laid eyes on him.

"Yeah, I didn't. I just can't put the pieces together. It's like something's nagging at my gut and I just can't tell what it is."

"I guess that's your investigative instinct taking over."

"Probably. You, on the other hand, look like you'd been sleeping for days on end. But, judging from your chipper mood, I know you well enough now to know that something's been cooking in that pretty head of yours. Lay it on me." He beckoned with his hands, palm-sides up.

"You're a smart man, Pascale Lupin. Or I'm an open book." She smiled then continued. "I managed to make a few calls last night, set a few things in motion, and we're pretty much ready to go."

"We are? Wow, I've got to give it to you, you never cease to surprise me. I see you also managed to find a coat to conceal the painting canister. I guess I can retire with a piña colada somewhere and leave you to it." He smiled and winked before he continued. "So, what's the plan?"

"Not here." She glanced at her watch. "In fact, we had better get a move on or we'll be late."

"Late? For what?"

Jorja was already headed to the exit where she hailed a taxi and gave the driver an address—paid with money Diego added to the bag.

Curiosity broke on Pascale's face. "It's on the not-so-nice side of the city. Why are we headed there?" he whispered, as the taxi started moving.

"I made a call to Andre last night. It was short notice but he managed to somehow come through for us and pull a few strings—or favors. I've already picked up a couple of items we're going to need in order to pull this off."

"Your Jamaican friend. Why does that not surprise me?"

"He's the best and he's all I have to work with considering Ben's off limits. I can't do this without his help, Pascale. Not with our small timeline."

"I get it. Perhaps I can shake his hand when all this is over." He briefly looked away before he turned to look into her eyes. "Sorry about Ben. It wasn't exactly planned."

"It doesn't matter anymore. There's nothing Andre cannot do or doesn't have a contact for, so we're good. And yes, maybe someday soon you can meet him. He'd like that," she said smiling.

When they arrived at the meeting point, she told the taxi driver to wait for them, then set off between two graffitied buildings, Pascale in tow. The derelict residential suburb was eerily quiet, considering it was broad daylight. Buildings with broken windows flanked their path and a putrid sewerage smell lay thick in the air. Following the directions she'd been given, she took a footpath that led to an abandoned water drainage pipe which ran underneath the train tracks. The pipe's thick concrete walls were decorated with more bright-colored graffiti that stretched all the way through to the other end. When they reached the pipe's exit, Jorja stopped just inside the concrete structure and glanced at her watch.

"Now what?" Pascale said, still in the dark over what she'd got planned.

"Now we wait."

"For what?"

"For our contact."

Less than a minute later a young Italian man with piercings that covered just about every part of his face walked up to the opening. His black-lined eyes that appeared even more deep-set than they would without the make-up, sized them up and down.

"You have the money?" he eventually said.

"As agreed, yes. Fifty percent upfront, the rest on completion of the job," Jorja answered.

"How do I know you're good for it?" the punk asked.

"You don't." She locked eyes with his.

"We're set for eleven o'clock." He held out his hand.

Jorja pulled an envelope from inside her waistband and handed it to him. He opened it and thumbed through the thick wad of notes before he stuck it inside the pockets of his far-too-tight jeans that somehow still managed to sag halfway down his bottom.

"I'll be in touch afterwards for the rest."

"Agreed."

The young man turned and disappeared up a grassy embankment.

"Who was that and more importantly, what did you just pay him for? And where did all that money come from anyway?" Pascale rambled off a list of questions.

"He's our red herring, and I told you I had Andre make a few arrangements for me last night."

Jorja turned and set off through the drainage pipe toward the taxi.

Pascale pulled back on her arm.

"Jorja, stop. I get that you're obviously in your element, and I even understand that you are used to doing everything on your own, but you have to let me in on your plans. We're in this together, remember?"

She knew precisely what his words meant and even in the shadowy confines of the underground pipe, Jorja noticed the pleading look in his eyes. Feelings of guilt suddenly flooded her heart. She had fallen victim to the very thing he had warned her about and it had snuck in when she wasn't looking. She had allowed the thrill of the heist to overshadow her spirit. The enemy had caught her off guard, like the roaring lion who prowls around seeking his prey, just as it warned in the Scriptures. She hadn't been vigilant, hadn't been on guard.

She covered her face with her hands and leaned back against the pipe. "I'm sorry, Pascale. I don't know how... I wasn't vigilant."

He took both her hands and clasped them together just below his chin then, lowered his eyes in line with hers.

"I get it, it's okay. Doing what we have to do here isn't easy, especially as believers. It's perfectly normal to fall into the enemy's devious snares. That's why I told you to watch out for it. I've been there, many times. But what's important, is that you recognize it and be on guard as we move forward."

She nodded then drew in a deep relaxing breath. As she let it out, she silently asked God to forgive her. She pushed herself away from the wall—and him—pacing a few steps away before she turned to face him again.

"This guy is our way in. Andre found him through one of his contacts. He and a couple of his friends have been pulling small thefts around Rome. Mainly targeting tourists, the odd gas station hold-up, and so on. They've been in and out of juvie for years and when this opportunity presented itself, they jumped at the chance to make some quick money. They are perfect for the task."

"And that task is?"

"They're going to break into the Vatican's secret repository. Of course, we know they won't actually succeed at it, but what it will do is create vulnerabilities in the Vatican's security measures. Normally, when a museum or institution like this has had a security breach of any kind, they have to notify their insurers."

"Yes, I'm aware. Insurance fraud protocols kick in and they have to do a full inventory on the insured items."

"Precisely. Protocol also states that each item needs to be re-appraised. That's where you and I come in. With our combined knowledge of art we'll easily pass as insurance officers. We'll make sure we start in the Pope's vault, that way we won't waste time. Then, once we're inside, we'll switch the real painting with a fake."

"And no one will suspect anything because who better to authenticate art than their trusted insurance appraisers."

He smiled. "It's genius. I can now see how you earned your acclaimed reputation."

Jorja ignored the compliment for fear of letting pride rule her heart again. "Genius but unfortunately still flawed. Andre wasn't able to find out who the insurance company is. Without that, he can't create our access passes or the forged documentation we're going to need to get in and pull this off. And we're fast running out of time to hunt down the company."

Pascale turned away, his hands on his hips. "I think I might be able to help with that. I have a contact, ex-girlfriend actually." He briefly made eye contact then looked away. "She's a clerk at a private investigations firm here in Rome. They often outsource their services to Interpol's insurance fraud division. She'll have access to that information for sure. She owes me a favor."

The space between them suddenly turned awkward and Jorja tried hard to ignore the fluttering sensation she suddenly felt in her stomach.

"That's great," she said, her voice suddenly higher than she intended. She cleared her throat. "How do you make contact with her?"

"Their offices aren't far from the hotel."

There was another awkward silence between them before they turned and headed toward the waiting taxi.

CHAPTER TWENTY-FIVE

T he taxi dropped them a few streets away from the office block and they made their way toward the building where Pascale's ex worked. When they entered the private firm's small foyer on the ninth floor, Jorja's stomach grew tense. *Stop acting like a silly school girl,* she said to herself, as they stepped up to the reception desk. But try as she might, she found herself increasingly more nervous with each second that passed. As Pascale enquired after his ex-girlfriend at the desk, Jorja was suddenly nervous to discover his taste in women. It was entirely ridiculous, she knew, but something between them was changing and she wasn't yet sure how she felt about it.

Nerves got the better of her and she finally said, "Perhaps I should wait outside."

But before she had a chance to turn around and run for the hills, a young woman with the body of a supermodel and legs up to her chin glided towards Pascale. Jorja watched as the girl's long slender arms eagerly wrapped around his shoulders before she lay two fire engine red lips on each of his cheeks. She was a gorgeous creature with deer-like eyes and pitch-black long hair that curled in perfect locks below her shoulders. Mesmerized by the girl's blatant beauty, Jorja suddenly felt self-conscious and greatly inadequate, and before she could stop herself—or make any sense of the emotions that now ran havoc inside her stomach—she made a feeble attempt at needing the washroom and dashed out of there.

When Pascale finally met up with her outside where she sat waiting at a small bistro table in the next-door street café, he had already wiped the red lipstick from his cheeks —and she had had time to regain control of her emotions.

Preferring to return her focus to their business at hand, Jorja was quick to ask, "Did you get it?"

Concealing the awkwardness that still lingered between them behind the rim of her coffee cup, she only briefly glanced his way.

He nodded and passed on the information needed to secure their security passes and the documentation.

"Excellent." She glanced at the time on her wristwatch then pulled a burner phone from the backpack.

"She doesn't mean anything to me, you know." Pascale suddenly announced.

Jorja's fingers fumbled with the buttons on the phone as she rushed off a text message to Andre.

"Who?" she pretended.

"Caterina. We had a brief fling many years ago, that's it, nothing serious. She's not the commitment kind and I wasn't looking for it either."

"It's really none of my business, Pascale." She dropped a banknote on the table and got up. "We need to get to the Vatican. It's nearly eleven."

Neither spoke of Caterina or whatever was happening between them again and by the time the city hopper bus dropped them in front of the Vatican, they had each decided not to push the topic any further.

They hovered outside the entrance to Vatican City, keeping their faces hidden from any security cameras and police officials. With the clock already fifteen minutes past eleven, melting in between the bustling tourists on Saint Peter's Square, they waited for signs of the arranged robbery.

"There's a chance they didn't go ahead with it, you know," Pascale whispered where he and Jorja pretended to pore over a few tourist brochures they had picked up on the bus.

"I know."

"Punk-kids like him are all about the money. I've seen it a million times while working undercover. And this kid is inexperienced and insanely greedy. I'm pretty sure he doesn't know the first thing about stealing a painting, much less have the know-how to make it disappear. We need to think of a plan B."

"Let's give it another ten minutes," Jorja said.

But, much to their relief, it took only half that time before the chaos erupted. Policemen scattered in all directions across Saint Peter's Square, charging between the disbanding crowd toward the city's main entrance in an effort to lock it down. Sirens wailed as police vehicles and security rushed to the scene.

"I feel bad for them," Pascale said.

"Who?"

"Those kids. We tricked them into another term in jail."

"I wouldn't worry about them. I bet you he's already talking himself out of it. If the police were actually quick enough to catch them. These kids grow up on the street and they're surprisingly resourceful when it comes to getting caught. Besides, they were only meant to trip the alarm, not steal anything. So, like I said, I have no doubt he'll get away with it."

"Is that what happened to you?"

A question formed on Jorja's brows.

"Growing up on the streets," Pascale clarified.

"No, at least not like these guys. I had Ben and later Andre." Her posture suddenly changed, as if she spotted something. "Follow me," she said as she hurriedly pushed her way through a clear spot between the thick crowd.

"Where are we going?"

"You'll see," she smiled back at him as she led the way until it became clear what—or who—she was chasing after.

"Well, I'll never," Pascale said as he got the punk-kid in sight.

They followed the studded youth as he hastily moved away from the gathering of people then slipped between the guards posted at the main entrance. As they too escaped the lockdown, they chased after him. Before long, he turned up into a side street. Increasing their pace they soon caught up with him and Jorja casually brushed past him from behind, then continued walking. Without any exchange of words, the youth quickly darted off in another direction.

"Keep walking and don't look back at him," Jorja told Pascale.

"Shouldn't we find out what happened, if they're okay?" Pascale queried, now walking alongside her.

"No need, they're fine. I've already settled what we owed him and that's that. We have, at the most, two hours to change into proper attire, get the paperwork done, and pick up the forgery. The Vatican will most likely act quickly to the security breach and they'll have the insurance send new appraisers by close of day. The longer it drags on, the longer they have to be closed to the public and the more tourist revenue they'll lose. We need to get in there asap."

"Copy that. What about the forgery? I'm sure we'll find a good copy at any of the other local museum shops, or even a gallery." He asked and answered his own question.

"It's already been taken care of. We just need to go pick it up."

Pascale stopped as Jorja sped a few paces on then turned to face him.

"Why are you stopping? We have to go."

He stood hands-on-hips staring at her. "You fascinate me, Jorja Rose. Do you know that? I mean, when, how? You've thought of everything and I've not left your side since we landed in Rome so, how are you doing it?"

Jorja closed the space between them. "Is this the undercover Interpol agent asking to lock me up again, or are you asking as a friend?"

"I guess the latter since I'm too deep into this now."

She smiled. "Andre's my right hand. It used to be Ben who coordinated everything but Andre has managed to step into his shoes quite nicely. All these little tricks, ways of communicating and passing money, et cetera, are like our own secret code of conduct. It's how we all do it. Did it," she corrected herself. "It's what guys like you would call the tricks of the trade. Like a sequence of events that play out on autopilot, set off by the one before."

"Like dominos."

"Something like that."

"So you call or text Andre, he makes contact with whomever and you just know how to execute the next step."

Jorja nodded.

"It's genius. If I'm ever fortunate enough to get my job back, I'd like you to come work with me. We can catch many a criminal with your inside track."

Jorja laughed. "Like my British mother used to say, 'many a slip between the cup and the lip'. Let's first make sure we get out of this alive and once we're on the other side, maybe we can talk."

"Deal."

CHAPTER TWENTY-SIX

Sixty minutes later, in the heart of Rome, Jorja and Pascale purchased two outfits that fit their newly claimed feigned profiles. Using the store's fitting rooms, Pascale changed into a tailored black pinstripe suit and Jorja a solid black pencil skirt, cream blouse, and matching black tailored jacket. She flung the art storage container over her shoulder and slipped the long coat back on to hide it. Looking like a modern-day Bonnie and Clyde, they exited the shop.

"All set?" Pascale said as they stepped out onto the busy sidewalk.

"As I'll ever be."

"What about the security passes and the documents? Has Andre sent through a pickup location yet?"

"A text came through about a minute ago. There's a street artist on the South side of the food market. A guy named Enzo."

"There're dozens of these artists all around the market. How do we know which one is Enzo?"

"He'll make himself known, don't worry."

Choosing to walk the short distance to the food market, Pascale cast a watchful eye over his shoulders. He was on high alert most of the time, but today, his insides were telling him to be extra cautious.

As they approached the bustling market, his eye caught a man watching them from between the food stalls and his stomach turned upside down. He leaned in towards Jorja.

"I think we're being followed," he said, then ushered her by the elbow between the tables of fresh produce.

"You sure?"

"No, but I don't intend taking any chances."

They zigzagged through the market, intentionally attempting to see if the man was doing the same.

He was.

"Yep, we're definitely being followed," Pascale confirmed.

"How many?"

"So far, just the one, but this place is packed with people so there could easily be more lurking around."

"Let's split up. You keep him busy, while I collect the package," Jorja suggested.

"I'll meet you back at the hotel," Pascale agreed.

They parted ways and Jorja quickly disappeared into one of the busier corners of the market while Pascale intentionally walked towards their stalker. As predicted, the man who had already lost sight of Jorja, stuck like glue to Pascale. Pascale deliberately lured the stalker away toward the North side of the market, giving Jorja ample opportunity to meet up with Enzo. But, as he found himself in a quieter spot, it soon became clear that the stalker wasn't alone.

There was a second one, flanking Pascale's left.

Pascale picked up the pace, his body tense and alert. Closer inspection had him recognize one of the men. He was the porter from their hotel. Years of experience told him they were hunting for the same bounty as the boat captain in Venice. By now his and Jorja's profiles would be all over the world and the porter had most probably identified them when they checked in.

The assumption brought him peace since it also meant they were amateurs. At least the porter was.

His friend? Not so much. A close-up look revealed he was carrying a gun beneath his far too small t-shirt—evident of the visible bulge in his waistband.

From across a compact row of produce tables, Pascale locked eyes with the armed stalker. It was another one of Pascale's tactical moves to show he was onto him, challenging him like a matador did his bull. The guy's nostrils flared as he pulled his hands into two tight fists next to his sides. He was ready for the fight too.

Pascale glanced over his right shoulder. The porter hovered next to a table of fresh tomatoes. He was easier to shake than the other one, Pascale thought.

He readied his body and casually walked along the tables of fruit to where there was a gap between the row of tables. When he was ready, he made his move and dashed across the market toward the center where it was most condensed. From behind him he heard a few shoppers shriek when the two huntsmen set after him and knocked several of them out of their way. Pascale's feet hit the uneven cobbled market square, darting between the produce-line aisles. His plan worked. The men chased him around like a cat did a mouse.

But while he had kept them off Jorja's trail, he now also knew that going back to the hotel was no longer safe—unbeknownst to Jorja who'd be walking straight into the trap. He'd have to somehow shake them and find her before she went to the hotel to meet him, he thought.

Deciding to risk it, Pascale ran toward the South side of the market. Behind him, the porter and his friend were still hot on his tail. He took a few deliberate turns, snaking between the stalls to throw them off his trail. It worked and when he was certain he had lost them, he made toward the Southend of the market in search of Jorja.

But, when he reached the small row of street artists, Jorja was nowhere to be seen.

It happened too quick for Jorja to react when the man's large hand closed over her mouth. The sweet smell of chloroform filled her senses as he pulled her into the van that appeared out of nowhere next to her. She tried putting up a fight but the ambush caused her to be too late to stop it. Soon her senses succumbed to the toxic liquid and her knees buckled beneath her. Moments later, everything around her went black.

P ascale skimmed through the row of artists. He had managed to lose the porter and his friend in a thick crowd of Chinese tourists but he knew it wouldn't be long before they catch up to him.

Out of time and out of options, he ran up to the first artist.

"Enzo?"

The gypsy-looking man shook his head and then pointed his paintbrush to a much younger guy sitting a few easels down the row.

Pascale darted toward him, ignoring the woman with her dog on her lap who sat posing for her portrait in his chair.

"Are you Enzo?"

"Who's asking?"

"My friend, she just came to see you. You had something for us."

The guy stood up and turned his back on his client as he pushed his bulbous nose in Pascale's face.

"Who's your friend?"

Pascale's heart thumped in his throat. Time was fast slipping away from him. Deciding he'd take the chance and trust that this guy was in fact their contact, he answered.

"Jorja. Andre arranged it."

The artist paused then answered, "I've not seen her yet."

Pascale felt the wind punched from his stomach.

"What do you mean she wasn't here? I just left her ten minutes ago."

Enzo looked back at his client and flashed the woman a fake smile before he turned his attention back to Pascale.

"Look man, I'm telling you, she hasn't been here yet. But, I've got what you need so just take it and leave me out of the rest." He waited for Pascale to respond but when he took too long, he turned around and dug a key from his bag on the floor behind him.

"Here, it's in a locker at the bus terminal across the street from Saint Peter's Square. If your friend pitches, I'll tell her you were here. Okay? Now, please go before my client goes to one of the other artists. Time is money."

He drove the key into Pascale's palm then casually turned to his client with comedic banter.

Shoving the key inside his pocket, Pascale frantically searched for Jorja through the crowd of shoppers. Every instinct in his body told him they had taken her. But he remained hopeful, prayed that he wasn't right.

He pushed his way back into the market, scanning through the people in search of Jorja—and the two bounty hunters.

But she wasn't anywhere.

Neither were the porter and his muscly friend.

As his heart pounded hard in his stomach, his mind raced with what to do next. Perhaps there was another Enzo. Perhaps this guy wasn't who he thought he was and Jorja was waiting for him at the hotel.

He ran toward a row of taxis that stood waiting on the edge of the market and jumped in the one closest to the exit.

"I need to get to this hotel as quickly as you can please? I'll pay extra." He shoved the hotel's business card and a large bill onto the driver's shoulder and locked eyes with him in the rearview mirror.

"I don't want any trouble," the driver replied.

"Here, I'll pay double!" Pascale added another note and pressed hard into his shoulder.

After a long pause the driver eventually said, "Buckle up," before he screeched the car into motion.

CHAPTER TWENTY-SEVEN

Jorja's eyes fluttered open as she slowly came to. The chloroform hadn't been strong enough to keep her knocked out. Perhaps it was intentional or perhaps her kidnappers were novices and had made a mistake, she thought, hoping it was the latter.

A slight bout of nausea caused by the chloroform lay in her stomach. She lay flat on her side, shaking back and forth as the van moved over bumpy terrain. Two male voices came from somewhere behind her but she chose not to look, not yet. As her body grew more alive she listened to them talking about horse racing and the bets they were going to place with their payoff.

Though desperate to make a move, Jorja held back, inspecting her surrounds first. The back of the van was dark, caused by the windows that were entirely blacked out with paint. Elated to discover neither her feet or her hands were bound, she cautiously panned her eyes through the darkness. She was alone in the back of the van.

When she was certain they were too deep in conversation to notice her, she quietly got to her feet, using the side panels of the van to keep her steady. Careful not to be spotted in the rearview mirror, she stayed back and assessed the two men. She recognized the passenger. He was the porter at the hotel. The driver, a much larger man, was unknown to her.

Her mouth tasted bitter as she contemplated her next move. To her left, a metal drainage pipe lay at her feet. The kind plumbers used. She could easily take them both down, she thought.

She took a deep breath, flexed her muscles and made her move.

With the driver focused on steering the car, she went for the porter first and wedged the pipe against his throat. She pulled his body back towards her, driving it deep into his headrest that pushed against her chest. Caught off guard, the driver swerved the van off onto the shoulder of the road, nearly losing control of it entirely. Jorja came close to losing her footing but she clung to the pipe that anchored her to the back of his carseat. Seconds later she had rendered the porter unconscious.

Knowing he was her next target, the driver flattened the gas pedal and reached for his gun. She swung the pipe across his face then knocked the gun from his hand. He moved to plan B and intentionally yanked down on the steering wheel. The car swerved wildly across the road. But his attempt to throw her off balance was futile and she whacked him over the head with the pipe.

He cussed at her in Italian, then shoved the back of his fist in her face.

Jorja fell back into the van. As the car swerved out of control, she somehow found her footing and went back to finish the job. This time, she yanked the still unconscious porter from his seat and pulled him between the seats into the back of the van. The driver tried to stop her from climbing into the front of the van and slammed on the brakes.

Jorja's body launched forward and crashed into the vehicle's dashboard. With her body twisted, she was quick to regain control and shoved her elbow back into the driver's face, then quickly followed with an uppercut before she finished him off with a strong right hook.

His body went limp on top of the steering wheel while his foot drove deeper down onto the gas.

She tried pulling him off the steering wheel but his body weighed too much for her to move even an inch. The vehicle sped down the road. Cars and motorbikes hooted and swerved in chaos out of the way. Unable to control the van, Jorja now pulled at his leg. But this too was too heavy for her to lift off the pedals.

Panicked prayers escaped from her lips as the van steered itself directly into the traffic and towards a large traffic circle with a fountain in the middle.

Realizing she had no way of stopping the out-of-control vehicle, she went for the door.

But it was too late and the van rammed into a car before it spun out of control and came to a grinding halt against the enormous statued fountain.

From the back of the taxi, Pascale impatiently tapped his hands on his knees.

"Can't you go any faster?" he eventually asked the driver.

"I'm trying but the traffic isn't moving."

The taxi slowed to a halt.

"Why are you stopping? Please, I have to get to the hotel," Pascale urged.

The driver threw his hands in the air. "I don't know what's going on but the traffic is backed up all the way to the *Fontana delle Naiadi*. It's not normal for this time of the day but there's not much I can do."

"How far is the hotel from here?"

"By car, about ten minutes down that way, but if the traffic—"

Pascale didn't wait for him to finish his sentence and was already halfway out the car.

He set off into the stationary traffic. Suddenly feeling hot and uncomfortable in the tight suit, he pulled at his collar to loosen his tie, then the top button. Urgency to get to the hotel before they ambushed Jorja pounded at his mind. The thought of them hurting her made his heart ache and he increased his pace. If he could get to the other side of the traffic jam he'd hail another taxi to take him to the hotel, he thought.

Following the way the taxi driver pointed to the hotel, he moved toward the front of the traffic where he eventually found it gridlocked around the large fountain that towered in the middle of the roundabout. Several people stood huddled in front of the traffic light and at first he thought of ignoring his curiosity. But as he got closer, a sinking feeling hit his stomach and he found his feet automatically veering toward the small group of onlookers. As he pushed his way through to the front, he noticed the white van upside down inside the fountain. The police hadn't yet arrived at the scene and no one did anything but stare at the accident scene. Unable to avoid the dreaded feeling in his gut, he moved toward the van, peering in to get a better look at who was inside.

Jorja's bloodied face lay wedged against the passenger side window.

"Jorja!" he yelled and moved to yank open the door.

It was stuck. He slammed on the window.

"Jorja, wake up!"

But she wasn't moving.

With his feet now wedged up against the frame of the car he pulled back at the door as hard as he could. His injured arm stabbed at his shoulder and nearly had him quit. In the distance, police sirens wailed toward him.

"Jorja, wake up, please! We've got to get out of here!"

Another yank and the door finally gave way. Ignoring the pain that shot through his arm he crawled inside the wreckage. With his body halfway inside the vehicle, hovering over Jorja to assess her injuries, he called out to her again. This time, her eyes fluttered ever so slightly.

"You're okay, you're okay, thank God," he said as he cradled her head.

The sirens grew louder. "We have to get out of here, Jorja, wake up."

He lightly tapped her cheek. Her eyes fluttered open.

"There you are. Can you walk?" he pulled her arm around his neck.

"I think so," she said quietly.

"Hold on, *amour*. I've got you."

It took hardly any time for him to lift her out of the car and carry her to safety. Behind them, the small group of onlookers started to turn back to their cars as an ambulance rushed to the scene. Eager to get out of there before they'd have to answer to the police, Pascale searched for a way out.

"Think you can make it to the trattoria over there?" he pushed his chin out to a small Italian restaurant on the other side of the fountain.

Jorja nodded.

Narrowly escaping the police, Pascale's quick thinking safely delivered them to a small table in the back of the restaurant.

Jorja's hand went to her head where a large red bruise showed evidence of a nasty bump.

"We should get some ice on that," Pascale said and called one of the waiters over.

"I'm okay." She moved to get up then fell back in her chair in a dizzy spell. "We have to get back to the food market. They took me before I could meet Enzo."

"I took care of it already. Just take a moment to gather your strength."

The waiter was back with a small bowl of ice.

"Could you also bring us two double espressos, please? Lots of sugar," Pascale ordered then wrapped the ice in his linen table napkin and pressed it against the bump on Jorja's head.

Jorja protested. "We don't have time for this, Pascale. If you managed to get everything we need from Enzo then we have to go, before the actual insurance agents beat us to it."

A look of concern flashed across his face. "Are you sure you're up to this, Jorja? Perhaps I should do this on my own. I can meet you here afterwards."

She shook her head. "It's not going to work. They always go in pairs. It's protocol."

The waiter set the two expressos down in front of them then left.

"I'll be fine, really." She smiled at Pascale. Her brow curled into a question. "How did you even find me?"

"I didn't, I mean, it was purely by accident. I was headed to the hotel and the traffic forced me to go on foot. I was curious like all the others, I guess."

"I don't know what I would have done without you there, Pascale. Thank you."

"I figure I owed you one. For saving me back at the plane crash. Now the score's even so let's keep it that way, shall we? No more brushes with death." He smiled.

But they both knew they couldn't make that promise, for they were not yet done with getting Diego his paintings. Nor did they know if he would spare their lives once they gave it to him. All they knew was that they had miraculously survived another fatal attack from the enemy and that God's hand was upon them.

But their moment of peace was short-lived and once again, danger came rushing toward them.

CHAPTER TWENTY-EIGHT

From the back of the trattoria, hiding in one of the corners, it was Jorja who spotted the muscled bounty hunter first. He had walked into the restaurant and stood looming at the entrance, his dark eyes searching through the diners.

Jorja's chin dipped onto her chest as she tucked her body deeper into the corner.

"Don't turn around. They found us," she warned Pascale, whose back was facing the entrance.

"How many?"

"Right now, only the beefy guy. It looks like he's alone."

"Let's wait it out."

Jorja agreed and held firm where she now hid behind the restaurant menu, praying that he didn't spot them.

But it was already too late.

Her eyes locked with their hunter's lurking eyes, sending shockwaves into her stomach.

"Too late," she warned when he came toward them.

"This way!" Pascale directed, already on his feet. He had already spotted the door to the kitchen in the back of the restaurant.

Jorja was right behind him.

So was their hunter.

A waiter got in the way and bumped against Pascale's injured arm, nearly popping it out of the socket again. But there was no time to stop.

Jorja slipped past Pascale, pushing through the crowded kitchen to clear his way. Pots clanked noisily to the floor, angry chefs shouted obscenities, screams echoed behind them as their hunter closed in on them.

When they finally reached the service door at the other end of the kitchen, Jorja and Pascale burst out into the cobbled alley and ran as fast as their legs could carry them.

As they turned the corner, they heard the service door slam shut behind them. The enemy wasn't far behind.

They pushed harder, fought their way to safety, prayed they got out of there alive.

Soon they ran into one of the busier streets and snaked their way through the manic traffic. Several times they got close to being run over, narrowly escaping an untimely death before they jumped onboard a passing tramcar and fused with the people of Rome.

"I think we lost him," Jorja told Pascale.

"And not a moment too soon. My arm is killing me."

She cast a concerned eye at Pascale.

"Don't worry, I'll be fine. But I'm not going to lie. I can't wait for this to be over."

"We'll get off at the next stop and make our way to the Vatican. Where's our security badges and the entry documents you got from Enzo?"

Pascale's nose crinkled. "He gave me a key, said it was in a locker at the bus terminal near the Vatican. Speaking of, do you still have the painting hidden under that coat of yours?"

"Safe and sound."

The trolley stopped and they hopped off.

When they were certain they weren't being followed, they hailed a taxi and made their way to the bus terminal. And, as arranged, the key unlocked what they went there for.

"It's all here," Jorja said as she scanned the contents of the envelope and the large printed copy of *Caravaggio's Nativity with St. Francis and St. Lawrence* that had been left for them. Shielded by Pascale's body, she rolled the painting up and tucked it inside the storage canister.

"We lost a lot of time. Think we're still okay to pull this off?" Pascale asked as she put her coat back on.

"No idea, but what I do know is that we're going to need to risk it. The sooner we get out of here, the better."

"After you, Mademoiselle," Pascale teased.

Remaining vigilant, it was a short walk to the Vatican where the main gates appeared to be closed off to the public. Outside, small groups of disappointed tourists huddled around their guides, cameras in hand.

"Ready?" Pascale said, straightening his jacket as they moved toward the security post.

Jorja nodded, smoothing her hair over the large bruise on her forehead. When they arrived at the security post, Jorja handed the forged paperwork to the security guard.

"We're here to do an appraisal," she announced, putting forward her best performance.

"Wait here, please." the stern-faced security member announced before he turned and disappeared inside his small office.

"Think he bought it?" Jorja whispered.

"We're about to find out," Pascale answered when the guard walked toward them.

"Badges please?"

They offered the guard their badges and watched as he scanned it with a handheld device.

Nerves gripped their insides as they prayed that the counterfeit badges would pass the test. The machine beeped. A red light blinked above the small screen. Jorja's heart leapt with fear. She tensed up when he briefly glanced at her before he scanned it again. In silent prayer, her stomach in knots, she pinned her hope on the card working the second time around. Next to her, Pascale's body was rigid and tense against her arm, his breathing practically absent.

The green light flashed on.

"Sorry about that," the guard said. "Sometimes the scanner glitches." He took Pascale's card and repeated the process. The green light blinked on quickly.

"All clear, follow me, please."

They didn't hesitate, grateful that they had managed to make it past the security. The guard led them to the Apostolic Palace's main gate where another pair of guards greeted them. A brief Italian exchange between the officials had the first guard hand over the entry document.

"You're early," the one guard said sternly as he skimmed the paperwork.

"Yes, sorry about that, we take our work very seriously and the quicker we get you guys up and running again, the better." Pascale was quick with an answer.

The guard's eyebrows pulled together.

"It says here you only need access to the private vault. Why not the rest of the Vatican as per usual? And where's Vincenzo? Why isn't he doing the private vault appraisal today?"

Jorja's heart skipped a beat.

"He was delayed with another matter at the office so we're standing in for him today since the situation here takes priority," Pascale answered.

"I see. Fortunately for you, His Eminence was called to an emergency press conference an hour ago, but in future, please stick to the scheduled time. My colleague will escort you into the vault room," he announced, then clipped the forged paperwork onto a clipboard.

"Thank you, won't happen again," Pascale said as the grim-looking guard stepped back for his colleague to take over.

"If you can follow me, please?" the second guard invited.

When he had ushered them through the Papal Palace, he led them into a small room that was, for the most part bare, apart from one red velvet antique chair that stood next to a second closed door at the back of the room.

"Please wait here," the guard instructed, then locked the entrance door behind him.

With their stomachs in their throats and tensions running high, they watched the guard talk into his two-way radio. When an answer came back, he turned to face them.

"You may enter the vault through that door over there." He pointed at a second door in the back of the room then continued. "There's a switch at the door when you're ready to come out, I'll be waiting here for you."

"Thank you," Jorja said.

As they turned to walk toward the door, the guard suddenly called out.

"Aren't you forgetting something?"

He looked suspiciously at them.

Jorja frowned. Pascale raised one eyebrow.

"Your gloves, it's protocol, remember?" the guard continued.

"Oh, yes, of course," Jorja was quick to respond. "We have them right here." She smiled and fumbled in her coat to find the pair of white gloves they had purchased with the suits.

"Got them," she announced then slipped them on as she flashed a nervous smile.

"Got mine too," Pascale waved his gloved hands in the air.

A nod of approval cued them to proceed.

On either side of the door above their heads, two surveillance cameras flashed tiny red lights as it whirred in on them. Holding steady under the obvious surveillance, Jorja pulled back on the door lever. The door hissed open.

"Wait," the security guard was suddenly behind them.

"Where's your registry?"

Jorja's heart froze as she snuck an anxious look at Pascale. She had entirely omitted that tiny, but important, detail of their feigned inspection.

CHAPTER TWENTY-NINE

With the guard's suspicious eyes pinned to the back of their heads, Pascale was quick to improvise and turned to face the guard.

"Our company has gone paperless, my friend. Something to do with the most recent G7 Summit. It's all about climate change and such. They expect us to memorize the inventory now. It's a lot of pressure but we've undergone extensive training. It's all locked up in here." Pascale tapped at his temple.

"Yes, of course, climate change is important. Please, proceed," the guard said, the expression on his face betraying his lack of knowledge on the subject.

Given permission to enter, the door sucked into place behind them as Jorja and Pascale stepped inside the Pope's private vault.

Pausing at the door, Pascale soaked in the ambience as if it were fresh ocean air, grinning from ear to ear as he instinctively scanned for security cameras.

"There aren't any," Jorja set him at ease, her tone suddenly dejected before it turned to sarcasm. "The Pope and his personal aide are literally the only two people who are allowed inside this vault and, since his royal robes are also kept safe in here, he often changes in here too. Can't have cameras capturing a half-naked Pope now can we? So, guess what? We're the lucky ones to be handed exclusive entry on a royal platter. A nice easy heist."

Pascale frowned. "Exactly, so why the tone? Aren't you even a little bit excited to be in here? Look at this place!" He twirled as he took it all in. "We're actually inside Pope Francis' private treasury, inside his palace! How many people can say that? And to think, we didn't even have to pick a lock to do it."

But Jorja didn't answer him and walked towards the painting she found hanging on one of the walls.

He pulled back on her arm. "Hey, what's wrong? Why the long face?"

"I just want to get this over with so we can get out of here, Pascale."

He let go of her arm.

"Sorry, I can only imagine how tough this must be for you."

"I don't think you can, Pascale. This was once my biggest dream, now it's become my biggest nightmare." She stopped in front of the painting and reached up to remove it from the wall.

"But you're here, inside the vault, appreciating all the beauty of what's inside. Isn't this good enough?"

Jorja stabbed the scalpel that had come with the forged paperwork into the corner of the painting and skillfully sliced the blade along the frame.

"Like I said, Pascale, you don't get it."

"Explain it to me then. I don't understand why you are so upset. Your dream came true, didn't it?"

She rose and faced him, her heart at turmoil with her head.

"Art thieves don't steal for the money, Pascale. They steal for the challenge, the thrill of conquering security systems, cracking impenetrable safes, getting away with priceless pieces of history no one else can get their hands on. Sure, the money is good, but it's the challenge that fuels the heist. And this one, this one would have been the ultimate, the unobtainable, the pinnacle of my entire career. Now, it's ruined."

Pascale stared into her watery eyes. "You're not that thief anymore though, Jorja. Let it go. That was the old you, the one you've been running from for twenty years. Don't get sucked back into it just because you're reliving the past. Sometimes God has a sense of humor. He takes you back to face what only He can set you free from before He gives you a new beginning. One that He already prepared for you. All these years you've been running away from your past, hiding, from yourself and from your scorned enemies. But you can't hide anymore, not from them, yourself, or from God. It's time to face your past head on, fight back. The sadness you're feeling right now, that's the final piece in the jigsaw, the piece that will fall into place when you fully let go of your past life and forgive yourself. Embrace the new you, Jorja. None of this matters anymore."

Jorja stared into his warm eyes. "What if I don't want to let go? What if all this has somehow reignited that passion, reminded me of what I once had, what I was good at? What if I can't let go?"

He cupped her face with one hand and wiped the lonely tear that had trickled down her cheek with his thumb.

"You turned away from it once, Jorja. Trust that decision. All this, it's just temptation knocking on your door, the enemy's one last stab at your soul. Resist it, Jorja. I've seen your heart, the real you, and you're not a thief. You're one of the good guys now." His lips curled into a mischievous smile. "We're fighting the good fight here, Jorja, so let's get this painting out of here and stay the course. God will correct the sins from the past. Let Him."

It took a while before she nodded but he was right. Her head was a mess, her heart an even bigger one. Grateful for his spiritual wisdom, silently asking God to give her courage and to keep her strong against the enemy's invisible snares, she shrugged off the past and turned her attention back to the painting.

I t took mere minutes for Jorja to carefully remove the original painting from its frame, but as she took the counterfeit copy from the storage tube, her heart sank into her stomach.

"It's all wrong!" she exclaimed.

"What is?"

"The size, it's too small for the frame."

She lay it down within the edges of the now empty frame where a four-inch empty border ran along the outer edges of the copy.

"Don't bother replacing the original, just leave it. By the time the Pope gets back to find it missing, we will be long gone anyway."

Jorja contemplated their options as she paced the small space in front of the painting on the floor.

"You're right. We'll be in Zurich in a few hours. The Pope is old, maybe he doesn't even notice the bare wall. We'll hide the frame behind the robe closet and hope for the best. Piece of cake," she said with jest then carefully proceeded to roll up the stolen canvas before slipping it into the storage canister. With the tube back in its hiding place beneath her long coat, Jorja smoothed her hair in place.

"Ready?" Pascale checked before pressing the signal button for the vault door to open.

In wait at his post, the guard let them out.

"Everything okay, I hope," he said.

"Yes, looks good to us. We'll be submitting our full assessment the moment we get back to the office. Oh, and just a reminder, protocol prevents access to the vault for the next twenty-four hours until the report has been finalized." Pascale turned then walked toward the exit.

The guard's expression suddenly turned suspicious.

"That's the first I've heard of it," he said, stopping them at the door.

Jorja held back, careful not to draw unnecessary attention to herself, her heart suddenly pounding. But Pascale kept his composure.

"Annoying, we know. All these new rules are making our work twice as hard but what can I say, we just do what we're told. I'll see if I can hurry the report along." He winked and patted the guard's shoulder.

A slight frown pulled between the security official's brows. He wasn't buying it, but before he could say anything more, his superior's voice sounded on his radio.

His brows pulled even closer together as his eyes instantly told them they had been made. The guard reached for the pistol on his hip as he took a few cautionary steps back before he aimed the gun at them.

"Put your hands up!" he yelled, the tip of his weapon aimed directly at them. "I said, put your hands up!" He repeated when Jorja and Pascale didn't react.

"Don't shoot," Pascale said. "I'm sure we can work something out here."

"I'm not interested. Move away from the door!"

They did as he said, their eyes pinned to the gun in his hand.

When they had stepped back against the wall that he had pinned them to, his other hand brought the radio to his mouth to announce that he had captured them.

CHAPTER THIRTY

A sideways glance between Jorja and Pascale silently synchronized their plan to attack. The guard's vigilant eyes darted back and forth between them. Another distress call came through his walkie, causing him to briefly lose focus on his prisoners.

Jorja didn't hesitate. With lightning-fast precision, she wrestled the gun from his arm, sending it flying across the floor. Disarmed, the guard lurched toward her, swinging a fist past her nose.

Pascale went for the gun.

Jorja delivered a right hook followed by a left hook before she finished the guard with an uppercut to the jaw.

He fell back to the floor, lights out with his nose bleeding onto his cheek.

Gun in hand, Pascale snatched the access pass from the guard's hip, unlocked the door then, popped his head out.

"It's clear but we won't have much time before they come up those stairs."

They ran towards the large staircase that stood between them and their freedom.

"Stop!" a guard yelled from the bottom of the stairs as he charged towards them.

"This way!" Jorja pointed to a door that marked the fire escape at the end of the long corridor and ran towards it.

When they reached the exit, they found it locked. Pascale scanned the guard's security pass. The door clicked open.

Behind them a small group of guards chased after them and they locked the door back in place.

On the other side of the fire escape exit, a narrow walkway guided them to an enclosed staircase that only led up. Out of options, they ascended, two steps at a time. Two flights up another locked door greeted them. Once more Pascale scanned the guard's pass.

The door remained locked.

Below them, in the hollow echoes of the staircase, the enemy burst through the first door. Frantic voices communicated back and forth on their two-way radios.

Pascale scanned the card again. Still the door stayed shut.

"They must have hierarchical access," Jorja announced as she searched for a way to open the digital lock.

"Stand back," Pascale yelled and aimed the gun at the lock.

He fired a shot. The lock exploded and the door sprung open.

Two flights down angered footsteps rushed up the stairs.

With the lock busted, they searched for something to lock the guards inside the building.

"Here!" Jorja wedged a single metal chair that stood to one side up against the door.

Seconds later it was clear who owned the chair. An armed guard rushed toward them, his eyes stretched wide as if they'd caught him by surprise.

He yelled something at them in Italian, aiming his semi-automatic weapon directly at their chests.

Adrenaline surged through their veins and their bodies reacted in flight as they ducked around an AC unit's metal housing. The guard opened fire. Bullets clanked noisily off the metal structure, inches away from them.

Desperate to find another way off the Vatican's roof, Pascale fired a shot back at the guard. The bullet hit the guard's leg, crippling him to the floor. Behind him the fire escape door flew open.

Jorja was first to run toward a small brick structure at the furthest corner on the opposite end of the roof. Shielded by the low bricked walls, she crawled toward the edge of the building and looked over the palace wall.

There was nothing but space dropping down to the ground below.

They fell back against the wall behind them, contemplating a way out. On the other side of the roof the guards were searching for them, the squeaky rubber from their boots betraying their positions.

With their bodies flush against the wall, hidden from the guards' sights, Jorja and Pascale curled around the structure. Markings of a helipad came into vision. On the far side of it, the thin arms of a metal ladder curled around the top edges of the roof.

With moments to spare before the guards would find them hiding behind the small roof building, they darted toward the ladder.

"You first," Pascale said to Jorja.

"But your arm, you can't climb down with one arm."

"Yes, I can, now hurry!" His voice was stern and commanding, jolting Jorja into climbing over the small ledge and onto the ladder. A few rungs down, Jorja looked up to find Pascale had already climbed over the ledge, his good arm curled around each step as his body swung in and out from the ladder with each descending step. A combined look of pain and concentration sat on his face as he maneuvered his way down toward her. Below them, a small courtyard grew closer. Jorja's feet hit the ground first. Above them, guards took aim. Forced to act quickly, she reached for the gun in the small of Pascale's back and fired two shots of warning toward them. The bullets hit the building in front of the guards' faces, forcing them to pull back.

Pascale dropped to the ground, groaning as he fell back onto his injured arm.

Jorja fired off two more shots, winning a small window of time for Pascale to get back on his feet. Quick to get away, they ran across the small garden courtyard, welcoming the roof overhang along the outer edges. A sanctuary—or prayer garden—of sorts, it was entirely enclosed apart from a gated doorway in the far corner of the garden.

"Over there!" Jorja pointed out.

Once again the door was locked and Pascale reached for the guard's security pass.

"Please work," he willed out loud.

The door clicked open, delivering them into a narrow, cobbled street outside the Papal Palace.

Relief flooded their hearts but, although they had made it out of the Vatican, they yet had to make it out of the Vatican City.

Loud sirens rang through the holy city as their feet hit the cobbles in tandem. Lost within the city's large walls, they aimlessly wound their way through the streets. Panicked onlookers had poured out of their homes and business, yielding curious stares at the fleeing couple.

But they kept running.

Soon they reached one of the large walls that surrounded the city. With no way out, neither up nor in either direction, they found themselves cornered.

"Now what?" Jorja exclaimed in panic, her eyes frantically searching for a way out.

"I'll hoist you up," Pascale said and signaled for her to get onto his knees where he had already assumed a seated position with his back wedged against the wall.

"It's no use, Pascale. The wall is too high. Not to mention how I'd get you over."

Forced to a stop, trapped in the narrow passages surrounding the Vatican City's high walls, they awaited their imminent fate.

And just as all seemed lost and doomed forever, Gerard Dubois' voice rang through the threatening air.

"Over here!" he beckoned from the shadows of a nearby alley.

"Gerard? What...how did you find us?"

"No time to explain, Pascale. Come on!"

Jorja and Pascale followed Gerard through a maze of narrow streets and into a building that was far more luxurious on the inside than it appeared to be on the outside.

"Dare I ask what this place is?" Pascale asked as they hastily followed Gerard through the grand residence.

"There are only about eight hundred people in the entire world who have the right to live inside these city walls, all of whom are prominent in their own right," Gerard said with pride.

"And you're one of them?"

Gerard stopped to look back at Pascale.

"I told you a long time ago not to underestimate my influence, Pascale."

The look in his eyes hinted toward far more that lay behind the simple words he spoke but neither Pascale or Jorja wished to venture there yet.

Instead, plagued by unanswered questions, they followed him into a two-car parking garage below ground where a shiny silver sedan stood waiting.

"Get in," Gerard ordered as he climbed in the front of the car next to the driver. "Get down between the seats and cover yourselves with the blanket."

They did as he instructed.

The car hastily wound its way through the narrow Vatican City streets as they lay hidden in silence.

"Stay still," Gerard commanded when security stopped the car at the city's exit gates.

Jorja and Pascale listened as the driver's window rolled down before he spoke to the guard. Whatever he said worked and the car slowly rolled forward. When they had passed through the exit gate, Gerard's voice came at them.

"You can come out now," he said when they were out of the guards' sight.

"You saved our lives back there, Gerard, thank you," Pascale said as the car set off through the busy streets of Rome.

Gerard didn't answer, instead, he dialed a number on his mobile phone and pushed it against his ear.

"Be ready, I've got them," he said before slipping the phone back inside his pocket.

But there was nothing liberating about the tone of his voice and a shiver ran down Jorja's spine. She glanced at Pascale. His eyes told her he had sensed the warning too.

And, when Jorja's eyes fell on the driver's face that reflected back at her in the rearview mirror, she instantly knew her instincts had not failed her.

Desperate to warn Pascale of the man she now identified beyond a shadow of a doubt, she motioned with her eyes for Pascale to look into the mirror.

When he did, and his body stiffened next to hers, she knew he had recognized the driver too.

Confusion washed over Pascale's face, his mind frantically racing in an attempt to put the pieces together. But no matter how hard he tried, there was no logical explanation why Gerard Dubois' driver was the beefy bounty hunter that had tried to kill them mere hours ago.

CHAPTER THIRTY-ONE

As danger buried its invisible fangs into their flesh, fear threatened to send the pair into panic and Jorja found herself reaching for the safety of Pascale's hand. He closed his hand over hers, gently squeezing her shaky fingers to let her know that it would be okay.

He pinned his focus on the situation. Years of undercover experience had taught him to keep his emotions hidden, to play the part and to not betray what he had uncovered.

"Where are we going?" He ventured, his voice calm and trusting of the man he had already spent years fooling.

"It's a surprise," Gerard snuffed.

Jorja shuffled uncomfortably and tightened her grip on Pascale's hand.

"Well, at the risk of sounding ungrateful, Gerard, we're sort of in the middle of something here. May I remind you that you signed us up to doing the impossible for your friend, Diego Cortez? And, as I predicted, it has nearly gotten us killed several times over. So, if you don't mind, drop us here so we can get to Zurich and finish the job," Pascale said.

Gerard turned to face him.

"I know, and we will get to Zurich soon enough, so sit back and enjoy the ride."

"We?" Jorja blurted out in surprise.

Once more Gerard turned around, his body now fully twisted back to face Jorja.

"Yes, *we*, Miss Rose. I have personally taken it upon myself to help you complete your mission." Gerard's eyes twinkled as his mouth curled up at one corner.

Pascale's hand moved to his gun. He could easily shoot him, he thought. But what good would that do? He had spent years of his life trying to catch Gerard Dubois in the act and this might just be the opportunity he'd been waiting for.

"You know, Miss Rose, Pascale told me that you were intriguing and I have to admit, you are nothing like I imagined you would be. Of course, I knew of your reputation long before Casanova here spotted you in the church back in Geneva." His eyes fell on Pascale's. "You never could resist a mysterious woman could you, Pascale?"

Pascale felt his blood boil, fought the urge to take Gerard down once and for all, right there in the car. Once more his hand subtly went for his gun.

"That would be a mistake, Pascale." Gerard's voice warned him, moments before he pointed a .357 Magnum directly at his chest.

"Hand it over," Gerard demanded of Pascale. "Slowly!"

The look in Gerard's eyes meant business and Pascale didn't hesitate.

"I don't understand, I thought we were on the same team," Pascale said as he surrendered his weapon.

"I don't think you know the meaning of that statement, Lupin. What's that thing they always say? Ah yes, you're a wolf in sheep's clothing."

"Takes one to know one," Pascale fought back. "I'm very certain Diego Cortez isn't going to let you live once he sees you for the traitor you are. He knows where we are, Gerard. He's been tracking us."

Gerard threw his head back as he bellowed a laugh.

"Oh, I wouldn't pin my hopes on Diego Cortez saving you. That scumbag's days were numbered."

"You killed him?" Jorja asked, her voice sounding less confident than she had intended.

Gerard smiled in confirmation.

"That's why you were on edge the day you introduced us at his house in Abu Dhabi. You were scheming behind his back," Pascale challenged.

"You're the outside man, aren't you?" Jorja said as the pieces finally fell into place.

Shock and awe was written all over Gerard's face as he looked at Jorja then Pascale. "She's a smart one, isn't she? I'd watch my back if I were you, Lupin. Judging by that look on your face she's even surprised you, hasn't she?"

He was right. Jorja had surprised him but he refused to acknowledge it and instead, Pascale let Gerard continue his twisted little game. Because, in the silence of his heart, Pascale had made a vow. He'd wait his chance until he had enough to take Gerard Dubois down and have him locked up for the rest of his miserable life.

"I have to say, Jorja, Züber had said you were the best he'd ever had but I don't think even he knew what he had in you. Pity things have turned out the way they have. You could have been very valuable in my business."

Pascale caught on.

"Wait, you were Gustav Züber's man on the outside, the one who intercepted Diego's consignment and sold off all his paintings."

Gerard's fat index finger went to the tip of his nose as he mimicked a throaty sound. "We have ourselves a winner," he mocked.

"And somehow, Diego Cortez was none the wiser. That's how you knew where to find us. He trusted you," Pascale continued.

Gerard squealed again as he held up a tracking device between his beefy fingers. "Give this man a trophy!" he mocked.

"Then why did you not just let them kill us back there? Why rescue us, keep us hostage?" Pascale asked.

"Because he needs us to retrieve the final painting," Jorja answered on his behalf.

"There she goes again, showing her master mind," Gerard said sarcastically.

"I always knew you were twisted, Gerard, but turning my own team against me, I'll give it to you, that was the lowest of lows."

Gerard's brows pulled into a small frown, hinting that he had no idea what he was being accused of. Desperate to find answers, Pascale kept at it.

"You are a greedy old man, Gerard Dubois," Pascale said, no longer able to contain the rage that was slowly bubbling to the surface.

"Actually, greed has very little to do with it, Pascale. Control is what I'm after. This is the only way I can get the controlling share in the Bouvier organization. You see, my old friend, Jacques Bouvier didn't quite have it in him to run a proper business. He was too caught up in the history and his passion for art. We were going to lose everything because he had a sudden attack on his conscience. I couldn't let that happen. I offered to buy him out but he refused."

"So you killed him," Pascale said.

"A man's got to do what a man's got to do. He left me no other option. It was genius if I may say so myself. Poisonous mushrooms and a crooked doctor can go a long way."

"Have you no shame, Gerard. He was your friend, you're Gabrielle's godfather! How can you be so heartless?" Pascale continued, his insides hot with fury.

"Gabrielle Bouvier is a woman and he insisted that she take up her birthright beside him in the family business. But she has even less business sense than her dead father. There's no place for women in my line of business. They get too emotionally involved and caught up in the details." His eyes went to their clasped hands to prove his point.

Jorja let go of Pascale's hand, suddenly reminded why she had cut Ben out of her life all those years ago.

Gerard continued. "But, unfortunately, they're a smart lot and, if men like us play our cards right, they can come in very handy. Until you don't need them anymore." Gerard's eyes narrowed as he stared into Pascale's eyes. "But then again, I don't have to tell you that now do I, Pascale? You know all about using the female species to get what you want."

Blood pushed into Pascale's head and suddenly his secret vow to let the situation play itself out lost the battle. He lurched forward and drove his fist into Gerard's face.

In reaction, Gerard's hand twisted and his finger accidentally squeezed back on the trigger. A single shot rang in the air.

The car jerked to one side. The driver's hand went to his shoulder. Blood seeped from his arm. As the car veered back and forth across the road, Pascale went for the gun in Gerard's hand, but when the driver suddenly regained his faculties and slammed on the brakes, Pascale launched headfirst between the front seats. The impact momentarily caused him to lose control of his senses and he slumped down between the seats.

Jorja readied herself to join the fight.

"Don't!" Gerard yelled, the tip of his gun suddenly close to her face.

Jorja stopped. "If you kill me you have no way of getting the final painting," she said, her eyes firm on his.

A small pause had Gerard contemplate her words before he turned the gun on Pascale.

"Perhaps I don't need him now that I have you, do I?"

Jorja watched as his index finger settled on the trigger and gently squeezed back on it.

"Okay, fine! I'll back off and do what you want! Just don't shoot him. I can't do this without his help."

Her hands were in the air as she slowly sank back in her seat.

"Pick him up!"

Jorja reached to pull Pascale back into the seat next to her.

"Try that again and I'll kill you both, got it?"

"You won't get away with this, Gerard," Pascale said, clutching at his injured shoulder as he slowly came out of the dizzy spell.

"Shut your mouth before I shoot you for real this time, Pascale."

"Fine, just lower the gun," Jorja said.

Gerard bellowed a laugh. "You must think me an imbecile. I know exactly what you're capable of and I'm not taking any more chances. Now sit back and keep your mouths shut."

Forced to do as he said, Gerard's gun holding them hostage in the back seat, Jorja and Pascale yielded.

But, when the car reached the outer skirts of Rome, more danger reared its ugly head once more.

CHAPTER THIRTY-TWO

The black SUV came from nowhere and slammed into the driver's side. Two, three times it came at them.

Shards of glass scattered in all directions as the final impact spun their car out of control, tossing it across the road as if it were a toy.

Pascale's body slammed against the seats then bounced back before he fell against the door.

Jorja came crashing down on top of him.

Another dizzying tumble had them airborne when the car rolled across the road.

Something hard hit the side of Jorja's face and the vehicle suddenly thudded to a standstill.

Out of breath, dizzy from the impact, Jorja heard Pascale call her name. She tried answering but couldn't. The sweet taste of blood settled on her tongue. A sharp pain stung at the back of her eye making it hard for her to open her eyes. She coughed as her lungs struggled for air. Pain came from everywhere. Conscious of her body lying awkwardly on a bed of glass, she tried pushing herself off the metal surface. But she was too weak.

In the distance, outside the car, she heard male voices. Footsteps rushed toward her. Movement sounded to her right. Pascale shouted at her to get out and run.

She tried but couldn't.

Again his voice came at her, frantic and pleading. Then silence.

Strong hands closed around her ankles, flipped her onto her back.

Her body dragged across the glass.

She forced her eyes open, caught a shadowy glimpse of someone who looked like Mo. A tiny ripple of fear fluttered inside her stomach before all reasoning washed it away.

In dreamlike state she fought against logic. It couldn't be him.

Defenseless and against her will, the hands dragged her body from the wreckage. She no longer heard Pascale calling out to her. No longer heard anyone. In one quick motion, sending sick into her throat, she was tossed over the man's shoulder like a bag of potatoes. Moments later she lay in a cramped, dark space before all awareness left her.

P ascale's eyes fluttered open. Pain shot through his entire body. His eyes strained against the darkness around him. Somewhere by his feet the tiniest beam of light broke through the darkness. He tried moving toward it, hit his head, felt the body next to him.

"Jorja," he whispered, now realizing they were in the trunk of a car.

She didn't answer.

He turned on his side in the hope of seeing her. Pain shot through his newly dislocated shoulder. He squealed into his fist until he caught his breath.

"Jorja, wake up. Wake up, Jorja!" His voice was pleading, desperate. Thoughts of her being dead crossed his mind and nearly sucked the life out of his body. With his feet he pushed himself up to where his head was next to her mouth, listened if she was breathing. Faint puffs of air pushed against his cheek. He shot up a prayer of thanks, asking God to keep her alive. With his healthy arm he reached across his body and gently patted her cheek, recognizing the stickiness that now settled onto his fingers.

"Jorja, *amour*, can you hear me?"

Silence.

The moving car bounced over the road, turned left, bounced a few more times, then stopped.

Doors opened then slammed shut. Footsteps circled the car. Voices in the distance. A woman?

Footsteps drew closer. Sharp light suddenly flooded his face. His hands went to shield his eyes, squinting to see who stood in the light.

Disbelief burst into his mind then settled in his chest.

But before he could say anything, a fist drove into his face and rendered him unconscious.

W hen Pascale came to, his body felt cold, his feet numb. As his senses slowly woke up to his environment, he learned he was on a floor. Cold pushed into every cell and bone in his body. It was bittersweet; numb from the cold but equally numbing the pain he had felt earlier—even his dislocated shoulder no longer caused him agony.

As he stretched out his palms, his fingers brushed over a thin layer of ice. It was as if he was in a large ice box. Straining against the cold, fighting with every ounce of strength he had in him, he pushed himself up off the hard, cold floor. But his legs were weak and he dropped onto his knees.

Ignoring the stinging behind his eyes, he took in his surroundings. It was a cabin, empty and partially lit by the bright light that burst through the slits between the timber that covered the single window.

His eyes searched across the floor around him.

"Jorja," he whispered. "Jorja!" he called out louder.

But she was nowhere to be seen.

He forced the life back into his limbs and pushed himself toward the door, yanking back on the knob. It was locked.

He slammed on the door.

"Hello! Help, somebody help me!"

Instinctively he knew it was futile but he tried again. Still no one came to his rescue.

Panic surged through his icy body as his thoughts ran away with him. What have they done with Jorja? She was alive when she lay next to him in the car but what if she didn't make it?

He fought back the sadness that suddenly threatened to engulf him and rushed toward the window instead. But it was no use. It was entirely boarded up from the outside.

Through the slats he could see snow, lots of it, everywhere. He listened. Bells chimed in the distance, the kind worn by mountain goats. He was in the Alps.

Outside, footsteps crunched in the snow toward the cabin. The door rattled and Mo was suddenly in front of him.

"Why are you doing this, Mo? Why have you betrayed me and where's Jorja?"

Mo's gun held Pascale in place, his eyes dark and threatening where he stared back at Pascale.

"We all have our reasons. I did what I had to do to get out of the Program, to be free."

"You think you're free? You will never be free as long as you have someone else to answer to, Mo. You should have come to me. I could have helped you."

"Shut up! You're not my boss anymore. Put these on and move."

Mo shoved a pair of boots against his chest, his gun pointed firmly at Pascale's head. When the boots were on his feet, Mo pushed Pascale toward the open door and out onto the thick snow.

"Walk."

"Where's Jorja?"

"She didn't make it."

Pascale dropped to his knees, sinking into the thick snow as first grief, then anger overwhelmed him.

"Why? Why would you kill her, Mo? She didn't deserve this and you know it."

Tears pooled in his eyes and streamed over his cheeks as his chest tightened and pushed into his throat. Slumped forward in the thick snow, Pascale Lupin's heart broke into a million pieces and sucked the life out of his soul. He no longer cared about Gerard or bringing the *Gardiens* down. Suddenly life had no meaning. Not even a life with God. Years of sacrifice, duty, perseverance to fight for what he thought was right exploded into nothingness. Guilt would rule his heart forever.

"For what it's worth, we didn't kill her, Pascale. She tried to get away and ran across the lake. There was a crack in the ice. We looked for her but—"

"You killed her, Mo. Who's behind this, huh?" Pascale was suddenly back on his feet, his eyes angry and filled with hatred. "Answer me! Who's pulling your strings, Mo? Who's this Geppetto that now owns your soul?"

The back of Mo's hand whipped across Pascale's face and sent him face-first into the snow.

"Let him go!" the female voice echoed in the crisp air.

Crimson liquid stained the white snow under his face as Pascale pushed himself upright. He knew that voice.

"Get him inside," she barked another order at Mo.

Mo reacted, shoving Pascale toward the large cabin that stood several yards away.

"You're going to pay for this, Mo. I'll make sure of that," Pascale threatened as Mo pushed him up the stairs onto a wooden porch and inside the luxurious cabin.

To his right, Gerard's corpse lay on the floor. Next to him, the body of another male victim whom Pascale could only assume was the owner of the final painting.

When Pascale's eyes trailed to the center of the room, Gabrielle Bouvier's stark face and signature red lips looked full into his face.

CHAPTER THIRTY-THREE

"Hello, Pascale," Gabrielle's voice greeted him as if she was welcoming him home after a long day's work.

Bile pushed into Pascale's mouth.

Mo forced him down into a nearby chair and stepped six feet away, his gun still holding Pascale hostage.

"You're as surprised as Gerard was before I put him out of his misery. Didn't think I had it in me, did you? Little Gabrielle Bouvier, the spoilt little rich girl who inherited her brilliant father's entire empire but isn't good enough to run it. An heir by birthright but not smart enough to step into her beloved father's footsteps. Yet, here I am."

Pascale remained silent. Apart from the sick feeling in his stomach, he was devoid of any emotion. He had no more battles to fight and, as far as he was concerned, had already lost the war.

"So, are you going to make me torture you or are you going to be smart and surrender?"

Pascale frowned.

"Quit the games, Pascale. This isn't an Interpol interrogation where you bluff your way through getting what you want. Where are the other two paintings?"

Suddenly his emotions were back and a smug smile broke on Pascale's face.

"I guess your genius mind didn't quite think all this through, did you?"

Her designer heels glided across the floor toward him. Towering over him, she tried again.

"Gerard also thought he could outwit me, Pascale. It cost him his life. Don't make the same mistake he did."

"You and Gerard are one and the same, Gabrielle; two dogs fighting over a bone. Tell me, was it worth it?"

"I am nothing like Gerard. He conned my father into doing his dirty work for him, smeared the Bouvier name without a care in the world. But he went too far when he killed my father and tricked the world into thinking he died of ill health. Gerard Dubois was a crooked, greedy narcissist who, like all the other men in this world, made the fatal mistake of thinking I am only worthy of throwing parties and running benefits. Turns out you're all wrong. I pulled your strings like a puppet master, carefully biding time until I saw fit to restore the Bouvier name and everything my father had worked so hard for."

"And I am nothing but collateral damage, right?"

"You got in my way, Pascale. You just couldn't let those files go, could you? I had to stop you before you ruined my plan. Franz's files were intended to lure Gerard into a trap. And when Jorja suddenly fell into my lap, I took the opportunity to return the Bouvier name to its rightful place in the world of art. These paintings aren't just worth millions, they are historical masterpieces, and who better to resurrect them and restore my father's name?"

Gabrielle turned to the side, lit a cigarette and puffed out a large cloud of smoke as if she had already received victory over all.

"Just a pity it's too late for that," Pascale said as he fought the reminder of what he'd lost.

His words had Gabrielle spin around to face him, confusion set on her face.

"It's never too late, *amour*. Tell me where those paintings are or—"

"Or what, Gabrielle? You'll kill me? Bravo, that ought to do it. Go on then, kill me. You have already stripped me of everything that mattered to me. But you're too late. Your evil, deceitful will to prove yourself has cost you the very thing you chased after. Your father's name, your name, the entire Bouvier Foundation is destroyed, revealed as the dishonorable thieves and murderers you are! You will never get your filthy hands on those paintings because they sank to the bottom of the lake when you killed Jorja!"

The blood drained from Gabrielle's face as Pascale's words registered. In an emotional fit of rage she screamed so loud it nearly burst Pascale's eardrums. Before there was any stopping her, she snatched the gun from Mo's hand and fired it at a nearby mirror before she aimed it at Pascale. Tears lay on her cheeks, anger had smothered her heart to where there was nothing but pure evil left in her eyes.

And as she moved to kill the last man who would ever doubt her power again, another gunshot blasted into the rafters.

Stopped in her tracks, Gabrielle spun around to find Jorja pointing a hunting rifle directly at her head.

"Drop your gun," Jorja ordered, her voice trembling under her wet, shivering body.

"Jorja!" Pascale yelled. "You're alive!" He was up on his feet but Mo's strong arm came across his chest and held him down into the chair.

Like two cowboys in a deadly gun showdown, Jorja and Gabrielle locked eyes and guns, each silently daring the other to shoot. But misguided hope fueled Gabrielle's mission anew.

"Hand over those paintings, Jorja, and you can both walk away from this alive."

"No," she replied and gripped the rifle even firmer between her frozen fingers. Her heart thumped in her chest, knowing that she could never pull the trigger. She was many things, but never a cold-blooded killer. Not even if it were her enemy. "The paintings are worthless, Gabrielle. It's over. You don't have to do this. There are other ways of reinstating your father's name. Killing us isn't one of them."

"I don't believe you. Now, where are they?"

"She's telling the truth," Pascale said. "She had it strapped to her body. There's no way it could have survived the water. It's over, Gabrielle."

The gun shook in Gabrielle's hand, declaring her emotions were running wild within her.

"You don't get to tell me that it is over, do you hear me, Pascale? I decide when it's over!" The gun wagged uncontrollably back and forth as she spat at him.

Dread sat in the back of Jorja's mind as she silently prayed. *Father God, don't let her do this. Don't make me have to shoot her. I don't want to have to pull this trigger. Grant me the wisdom to say what you need me to say.*

And, in a final desperate attempt to persuade Gabrielle to surrender, Jorja put her trust in God and tried once more.

"It's not too late to turn your life around, Gabrielle. We've all done things we shouldn't have but you have a chance to make things right. This doesn't have to end in more death."

A hysterical giggle escaped from Gabrielle's mouth.

"Funny, that's exactly what my priest told me. Newsflash, this isn't a confession box and even if it were, God gave up on me a very long time ago." Sadness laced Gabrielle's voice.

"I don't believe that. We all sin but God desires everyone to come to repentance and if that's what you want, you will be justified by His grace, through His son, Jesus. God forgives those who seek His forgiveness. All you have to do is ask."

And, as Jorja said all she could say, Gabrielle's gun still aimed at her chest, she watched as God worked a miracle in Gabrielle's heart.

The gun dropped to the floor next to Gabrielle's feet as tears streamed down her flushed cheeks. When she turned to face Pascale, her eyes spoke of regret and shame for what she had done.

"It's over, Mo. Let him go."

Mo did as she said and took the opportunity to run for the hills, run to his newfound freedom—whatever that meant.

Jorja lowered her gun and fell exhausted to the floor, still drenched in the freezing waters of the icy lake. As her mind caught up with all that had passed, all her guilt, her search for freedom, God worked a miracle in her heart too.

For in that moment, as Gabrielle surrendered defeat and Pascale held Jorja in his arms, she knew that she had already been redeemed and, that no matter how deep and perilous her valleys may be, God alone had the power to remove them.

Nothing she did to atone for the sins of her past, could ever set her free. For it was through God's gift of grace alone that the shackles of her past would no longer hold her captive.

It had taken everything she had and nearly took her life, but she had made it through the perilous claws of darkness and stepped into the blissful light of forgiveness, fully redeemed.

P ascale pulled his coat's collar over his neck as he stepped out onto the sidewalk to take a call. Away from the crowded foyer of the National Gallery in London, he listened to the voice on the other end of the line.

"Thanks for keeping me posted," he eventually said. "I'll send my final report through as soon as I can."

When he had finished the conversation and hung up, Jorja walked toward him.

"Is something wrong?" She asked where she now stood next to him.

"I'm sorry, *amour*," Pascale replied, planting a gentle kiss on her forehead. "I know we agreed not to let anything interrupt our special night, but that was the office calling with an update. As it stands, they've not found them yet.

They discovered Kalihm's car in the alley behind Franz's club, but there was no sign of him. They found blood in the trunk, but not enough to imply that he might be dead. The trunk door was busted open from the inside, so probably he escaped and is in hiding somewhere. As for Harry? Well, as expected, he left no trace behind. A man with his skills has long since disappeared underground. The dark web is, after all, his territory."

"What about Mo? He couldn't have gotten far after he fled the cabin. Especially with that snowstorm that hit the next day."

Pascale chuckled. "Don't be surprised. Mo's ability to pull through any circumstance is one of the reasons I selected him in the first place. He can survive anything, even a snowstorm. Trust me, if he really wanted to, he could hide out in a mountain cave for decades."

"So what happens now? Are you thinking of going back to Interpol?" Jorja asked with trepidation.

Pascale pulled her into his arms. "And leave you behind in St. Ives? Never, *mon amour*. I'm never letting you go. Besides, rumor has it that the local police station is short a man. My transfer paperwork is already underway." He cupped her face. "So, do you think St. Ives is ready for me?"

Jorja smiled widely. "More than ready."

"Well then, what do you say we get back inside and enjoy the unveiling? If I recall, I promised you I'd give those paintings the justice they deserve."

Jorja nodded and followed him back inside. And, as she settled into the seat next to Pascale to watch the ceremony, pure joy overwhelmed her. For the first time in her life, she felt at peace. Whole, fully forgiven, and firm in the knowledge that the peace that had once felt so far off had now found its way into the deepest corners of her heart and soul.

For all have sinned and fall short of the glory of God,
and all are justified freely by His grace
through the redemption that came by Christ Jesus.
Romans 3:23-24

Thank you for reading! **Get your free and exclusive Valley of Death Fact File** with character inspiration, locations, and research!
Bonus: Take a closer look at the scriptures that inspired each book along with **Biblical insights**
Added Bonus: A super exclusive sneak at my **plotting board**!

Get Valley of Death Fact File
(https://freebies.urcelia.com/vod-fact-file)

You can also visit my online store
(https://shop.urcelia.com)for exclusive discounts,
merchandise, and promotions on my books.

**I appreciate your help in spreading the word,
including telling a friend. Reviews help readers
find books! Please leave a review on your
favorite book site.**

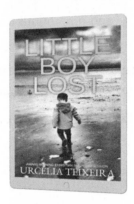

MORE BOOKS BY URCELIA TEIXEIRA

Angus Reid Mysteries series
Jacob's Well
Daniel's Oil
Caleb's Cross

Adam Cross series
Every Good Gift
Every Good Plan
Every Good Work

Jorja Rose trilogy
Vengeance is Mine
Shadow of Fear
Wages of Sin

Alex Hunt series
The Papua Incident (FREE!)
The Rhapta Key
The Gilded Treason
The Alpha Strain
The Dauphin Deception
The Bari Bones
The Caiaphas Code

PICK A BUNDLE FOR MASSIVE SAVINGS exclusive to my online
store!
Save up to 50% off plus get an additional 10% discount coupon.
Visit https://shop.urcelia.com

More books coming soon! Sign up to my newsletter to be notified of new releases, giveaways and pre-release specials.

MESSAGE FROM THE AUTHOR

**All glory be to the Lord, my God who breathed
every word through me onto these pages.**

*I have put my words in your mouth and
covered you with the shadow of My hand*
Isaiah 51:16

It is my sincere prayer that you not only enjoyed the story,
but drew courage, inspiration, and hope from it, just as I
did while writing it. Thank you sincerely, for reading
Wages of Sin.

**I appreciate your help in spreading the word,
including telling a friend. Reviews help readers
find books! Please leave a review on your
favorite book site.**

Writing without distractions is a never-ending challenge. With a house full of boys, there's never a dull moment (or a quiet one!)

So I close myself off and shut the world out by popping in my earphones.

Here's what I listened to while I wrote *Wages of Sin*:

- 10 Hours/God's Heart Instrumental Worship—Soaking in His presence (https://youtu.be/Yltj6VKX7kU)
- 2 Hours Non-Stop Worship Songs—Daughter of Zion (https://youtu.be/DKwcFiNe7xw)

When I finished writing the last sentence of the book!

How great is our God—Chris Tomlin

(https://youtu.be/KBD18rsVJHk)

ABOUT THE AUTHOR

Award winning author of faith-filled Christian Suspense Thrillers that won't let you go!™

Urcelia Teixeira, writes gripping Christian mystery, thriller and suspense novels that will keep you on the edge of your seat! Firm in her Christian faith, all her books are free from profanity and unnecessary sexually suggestive scenes.

She made her writing debut in December 2017, kicking off her newly discovered author journey with her fast-paced archaeological adventure thriller novels that readers have described as 'Indiana Jones meets Lara Croft with a twist of Bourne.'

But, five novels in, and nearly eighteen months later, she had a spiritual re-awakening, and she wrote the sixth and final book in her Alex Hunt Adventure Thriller series. She now fondly refers to *The Caiaphas Code* as her redemption book. Her statement of faith. And although this series has reached multiple Amazon Bestseller lists, she took the bold step of following her true calling and switched to writing what honors her Creator: Christian Mystery and Suspense fiction.

The first book in her newly discovered genre went on to win the 2021 Illumination Awards Silver medal in the Christian Fiction category and the series reached multiple Amazon Bestseller lists!

While this success is a great honor and blessing, all glory goes to God alone who breathed every word through her!

A committed Christian for over twenty years, she now lives by the following mantra:

"I used to be a writer. Now I am a writer with a purpose!"

For more on Urcelia and her books, visit www.urcelia.com

To walk alongside her as she deepens her writing journey and walks with God, sign up to her Newsletter - https://newsletter.urcelia.com/signup

or

Follow her on

Facebook: https://www.facebook.com/urceliabooks

Twitter: https://twitter.com/UrceliaTeixeira

BookBub: https://www.bookbub.com/authors/urcelia-teixeira

 facebook.com/urceliateixeira
twitter.com/urcelia_teixeira
instagram.com/urceliateixeira